I0597394

Patron of Joy

R. A. EMERSON

EMERSON
CLEAN FICTION AUTHOR

DEDICATION

This book is dedicated to my lovely wife Lori who demonstrates infinite patience with me every day. Without her love and support, none of this would be possible.

CONTENTS

CHAPTER ONE

The steady bump, bump feel of the tires was comforting as the private jet rolled down the runway toward an on-time departure. Victoria was tired and looking forward to getting home. Not that she had anyone to go home to. Unless you counted Carter, but in Victoria's opinion, he was kind of an ass. The bumping stopped as the plane lifted off and the landing gear retracted. It comforted Victoria knowing they were safely in the air. Only a few more hours and they would be home. She glanced out the window and saw the clear night sky. With any luck, they would have clear skies for the rest of the trip. But they wouldn't be quite so lucky.

She looked to her left and saw her father in the seat next to her. He looked back and gave her a warm smile. Normally he flew the plane, something he enjoyed, but this trip was too far for him to do alone, so he split the duty with Derek, a hired pilot who had the controls for the last leg. Victoria smiled back, then quickly turned her head away. She knew that look in his eyes. He wanted to talk shop, and she was far too tired to participate. Too late.

"Boy, we really killed it this trip, didn't we?" he asked, already knowing the answer. Her father, James Van Hough, was the CEO of a company he built from nothing. Now, over twenty years later, it was a large, very successful company.

"Yes, we did," she said, keeping her answer brief, hoping he would stop talking and they could go to sleep. This had been a whirlwind trip to South America to find sources for coffee, nuts, and wine, and they did "kill it." Victoria, his VP of purchasing, frequently went with him on overseas trips to find additional sources of products for their import company, Van Hough Industries. She looked over at him and saw him waiting for more. Damn. "If we can get the logistical channels in place soon, it will add significantly to our bottom line for the quarter and the year." A big smile formed on his face. She knew he wasn't happy about the information; he was proud that his daughter was so smart and turning into such an amazing professional.

"I'm glad to have you back from school. These trips weren't the same without you. Your education will serve you well, but you have such an innate ability to know what will sell and what won't. When the time is right, you are going to make a perfect president for the company." He finished by reaching across the aisle and putting a hand on her shoulder and rubbing it. It was a fatherly gesture. They often had to walk a professional tightrope when working together. He was Jim during business meetings. They shook hands like other business executives. But during private times like now, he was Dad. They would hug, and he would show her affection, and she would do the same to him. Their father-daughter relationship had been very special for as long as she could remember. He was loving, patient, and kind. When he touched her shoulder, she felt closer than ever to him.

But Victoria was a strong woman and wasn't afraid to speak the things that were on her mind. After briefly enjoying the moment, she went to the subject that most annoyed her. "It's nice that you say that, Dad, and I know you mean it, but you need to work on Mom. She will not go quietly, you know that." Victoria knew this was a delicate subject, but she wasn't afraid to go there. Her mom currently occupied the office of president and her dad would have to make that change. She didn't have any actual skills and made few contributions to the company, Victoria thought, but she had been there for years. Her parent's marriage was almost nonexistent, making it even more difficult for her father to pull the change off. He may need a push to get it done, but she would wait for the right time. Now was not it.

"Speaking of your mother, how is Carter these days?" Jim asked with a look of concern.

"That's a strange way of referring to him, but he's fine. His usual self."

"You mean his self-absorbed, egocentric, narcissistic self? Honey, why don't you find someone who is right for you, not someone who your mother picks. He's not good for you. I tell you this as your father."

Victoria knew he was right, but it was too complicated. Her mother was way too interested in her life. She didn't just express her preferences, she forced them onto Victoria, and Carter was a perfect example. *Victoria dear, he's Harvard educated*, she had said to sell him to her. *Victoria dear, he's a VP in his father's company, just like you.* She had badgered Victoria until she'd finally agreed to see him. Her mother had even made the call and set up the first date. Which, of course, Victoria had had no knowledge of.

"Well, I know this is going to make me sound just like your mother, but if you ever want to meet a wonderful guy, I know him. He's perfect for you." Victoria turned her head and looked straight forward, letting out a long sigh. She knew her father was right, and any man who passed his scrutiny would be a great partner for her. And that was what she wanted: a partner. Unfortunately, she was not ready to go up against her mother. Alice was ruthless and it would be a battle. She had other things requiring her attention right now.

"No pressure at all. He's not expecting you to call. But

3

if you change your mind, his name and number are on here," he said as he slipped his business card into the side pocket of her laptop bag. Then he got up and walked to the front of the plane to talk with Derek.

Victoria turned to gaze out the window into the openness of the skies. The moon shone brightly, and it was easy for her to imagine being with a wonderful man. She wanted someone who would be a suitable partner with her. Someone who loved her and thought of her as an equal. That's definitely not what she has now, she thought. And with the mood broken, she reached down, retrieved her laptop, opened it up, and started working. There was so much to do after this trip and she needed to get started.

***

She was making excellent progress with her work when she noticed the first bumps of turbulence. They broke her concentration, but she quickly returned her focus to her work. The second bout was longer and more extreme, bouncing her laptop up and down on her tray. Victoria had flown on this plane many times, so she knew it wasn't unusual to experience some turbulence. She glanced out the window and noticed the clear skies had morphed into something that looked angry. The moon was still visible, and it illuminated thick clouds below and in front of them. The clear skies were gone.

Her father had slipped back into his seat while she was working and must have fallen asleep. The bumpiness hadn't woken him, and that comforted her. She checked her watch and determined they had about forty-five minutes of flight time left. They would descend soon, so she decided to use the restroom while she could still get up from her seat. She unbuckled and stood up at the same time as more jostling of the jet, causing her to drop her laptop on the ground with a crash.

"Damn!" she exclaimed as her father woke up from the

combination of bumps and noise.

"Are you okay?" he asked.

"I'm fine. It's getting a little bumpy, but we are almost there," she said.

Jim looked out the window and confirmed what she just saw. "Yeah, it looks like it's going to get pretty rough out there. I was reviewing the weather forecast with Derek earlier and we saw several large storms developing and heading toward home. It's gonna get a little hairy as we descend. But based on what we saw, we should be able to get in before the really bad stuff hits. We'll need to buckle up soon."

"Okay. I'm just going to the restroom first," Victoria said as she headed to the rear of the plane. Once finished, she headed back to her seat. As she got to one table, a violent wave of shaking hit the plane, knocking her into the table. She lost her breath as she rolled off it and hit the floor. In an instant, her father was unbuckled and back, helping her.

"Are you okay?"

"I just had the wind knocked out of me. I'll be fine," she said, still struggling to catch her breath and rubbing her side where the table dug in. He helped her back to her seat, then took his. They both buckled their seat belts for the treacherous ride to the ground.

There was a phone next to his seat, so her father picked it up and called the cockpit. Victoria could only hear her father's part of the conversation, but what she heard concerned her greatly.

"How's it going? I know, we're getting bounced around back here pretty good. . . . Can you find any smooth air? Damn . . ."

Lightning flashed through the cabin and rain began streaking across the windows. They were descending into the clouds and it was getting much worse.

Her father continued talking with Derek. "How long until they hit? Should we divert? Are you sure you can thread the needle between them? Do you need me to come up there and help you fly? Okay. Let me know if you need me." He hung up the phone and looked at Victoria. There was a look of grave concern on his face that most people would not have detected. But she knew her father, and she knew that look. Her palms got sweaty and her throat went dry. She waited for the news.

"It's not too bad," he said, obviously lying. "There are two storms coming in. They are too big to go around and too tall to fly over." Before he could finish, the plane made a sudden drop that caused her to feel her stomach in her throat and catch her breath. She dug her fingers into the armrest. After a few seconds, the plane seemed to stop falling.

"You know that happens sometimes. Don't be alarmed," he said, attempting to calm her fears. The plane nosed down again, but in a more controlled manner this time, and she eased up on her grip as he placed his hand over hers.

"Derek feels like we have just enough time to fly between the storms and land so we aren't going to divert." As the words finished, the plane shook violently, then banked hard to the right. Another flash of lightning illuminated the cabin. Her father was looking directly at her. "Victoria, you are going to be fine. Trust me." And she did, but she was frightened regardless. She was perspiring through her silk blouse, and her heart was racing.

Freefall again, except for much longer before the plane appeared to get back under control. Another bank and another violent shudder that caused the cabinets in the back to come open and spill glassware across the back of the cabin.

Jim unbuckled his seat belt and began getting up.

"Where are you going?!" Victoria yelled in a panicked, childlike voice.

"I'm going to see if Derek needs help."

"No!" Victoria yelled. "Please don't leave me alone!

Please, Daddy!"

He sat back down and buckled up again. "Okay, honey. I'm sorry. I won't leave you." He reached over and touched her hand again in reassurance.

The plane descended farther as the bumping and shaking became near continuous. Victoria's body ached from being tensed up and bounced around. She had never been so scared in her life.

Jim turned his attention to the window as another lightning flash lit up the cabin again with the rapid clap of thunder not long after. His eyes appeared to be glued to the ground. Or at least where he thought the ground should be.

"Come on, come on. We should be below the cloud deck now. Damn it." He picked up the phone to call the cockpit just as an exceptionally violent shudder hit, causing the phone to fly out of his hands.

"There it is. The lights . . . Wait . . . You're too low!" he yelled to the empty cabin. "Derek! You're going in too hot! PULL BACK!"

Once again, the plane dropped, this time hitting the ground so hard that it jarred Victoria's back. Then it seemed to bounce back up in the air again, lean to the left hard, then make one last drop to the ground below. This time, instead of wheels, she heard screeching. Metal scraping across the ground underneath her. It was impossible to tell if the plane was still going forward or sideways, but the sound was deafening and the shaking like nothing she had ever experienced before. After what seemed like an eternity, the plane stopped and there was a strange quiet within the cabin. Victoria had closed her eyes and ducked her head when the plane first hit the ground, and now she was stuck in this position. She could tell the cabin was filling up with smoke, but she could not move. Not because of debris or an obstruction, but because she was frozen by fear and uncertainty.

Then, through the ringing in her ears, she heard a familiar voice. "Victoria! Get out!" She looked up in time to see her father standing up. His face was bloody, but he was alive. He came to her and unbuckled her seat belt. "Get up!" He pulled her out of her seat, into the aisle and to the back of the plane. He opened the door and jumped to the ground. "Come on, honey! I've got you!" And he extended his arms out to her. She jumped. It wasn't far, but her legs could hardly support her weight and they tumbled to the ground. Strange. They were in grass. Wet grass. The rain poured over them and the wind made howling noises. Lightning flashed all around them. Jim got up and helped Victoria to her feet, directing her a safe distance from the plane.

"I'm going back in!" he said over the noise of the storms.

"No! Daddy, don't go!"

"Derek is still in the plane. I have to see if he's alive. Stay here! I'll be right back."

With that, he headed back to the plane. With the help of the lightning, she could see that the plane appeared to be in one piece but was clearly smoldering. She watched as her father disappeared back inside the plane. She looked at her watch. One minute. Two, then three. "Come on, Daddy!" she said to herself. Four minutes. Tears came out of her eyes and mixed with the rain that continued to pour down. Finally, she saw movement at the door and her father jumped to the ground. He reached up and pulled what appeared to be a body from the plane. The body seemed lifeless as it was hoisted on her dad's shoulder. He struggled with the weight and had to put it down on the grass. He took both arms and dragged Derek across the grass near Victoria, and she met him to help pull him to safety.

"Is he alive?" she asked, afraid of what she might hear.

"Yes, but he seems to be badly injured."

He moved around to kneel next to Victoria and put his arms around her, holding her tight. She wept uncontrollably as the sounds of emergency vehicles filled the night.

CHAPTER TWO

Her alarm went off and Victoria gingerly rolled over to silence it. It was Saturday, and she was never so happy to see the weekend. Yesterday was the first day after the accident that saw her father's beloved plane destroyed in a grassy field, just off the runway where he had landed it many times before. She found out late last night that Derek had several broken bones and a concussion but would make a full recovery. She was grateful for that. Her father had some bumps and bruises. Other than being sore, Victoria escaped without injury. Thinking back, she still could not believe what had happened.

Friday was a workday, but after the unfortunate events of the prior day, she called in sick. They would all have to understand. She spent the day in her bedroom suite, sleeping, watching television and reorganizing her ginormous closet. It needed to be done, and it was the perfect thing to get her mind off the crash. Besides, she needed to make more room for new acquisitions. One thing that Victoria enjoyed more than any other was to shop. She purchased clothes, shoes, handbags, jewelry, and anything else that caught her eye. Her closet showed it. Bigger than the master bedroom in most homes, her closet was wall-to-wall shelves, drawers, hanging areas, and cubbies to display her nearly sixty pairs of shoes. There were several full-length mirrors, a makeup station, and an island topped off with a beautiful crystal chandelier.

Victoria slid out of bed and made her way through the closed doors and around the piles to the island. The closet looked as if her father's plane had crashed inside of it. Clothes were strewn everywhere, two small piles of shoes to the side and a half dozen handbags lined up near the double entry doors. Victoria was proud of the progress she made.

She opened several drawers and after a few minutes, selected her outfit for the morning. She was going out later tonight and the thought of that made her sigh loudly, but she would worry about that later.

Since returning home from school six months ago, she hadn't had the time to clean, organize, or shop. But after her near-death experience, she vowed to start making time for the things she liked most. She just wished the rest of the world was on the same page with her new life plan. All day long yesterday, work interrupted her: phone calls, emails, and requests to join various conference calls. She found herself falling back into her old work habits and had to continuously remind herself of the new Victoria.

She dressed, put on a little makeup, fixed her hair, and settled back on her bed, just in time to hear the knock at her door. Instinctively, she rolled her eyes. Over the last day and a half, she hadn't left her room. During that time, she took all meals in her suite. Each one brought to her by Helen, the most senior member of the household staff and her mother's right hand. Each time, Helen, at her mother's insistence, strongly suggested that Victoria join her mother in the dining room for a meal. Each time, Victoria sent her away with a "no." She liked Helen, but knew that, in the end, she was her mother's eyes and ears in the house. Any and everything eventually ended up going back to her mother. This was a hard lesson learned over many years.

"Come in, Helen," Victoria said and as the door opened,

she anticipated seeing her conservatively made-up face, well-coifed hair, and perfectly pressed uniform.

"What? Helen, who?" came the voice of her father as he rounded the door into her suite.

After recognizing her father's voice, excitement welled up in her and she jumped out of bed to greet him. As soon as he cleared the door, Victoria wrapped her arms around him and gave him a hug. He recoiled slightly and groaned as she squeezed, causing her to release her grip and take a step back, looking at him with concern.

"Sorry, Victoria, I'm still really sore."

"Sorry, Dad. I didn't realize you hurt so much."

There was an unusual pause to the conversation as her father cocked his head to the right as if listening to some inaudible sound in the hallway. "Don't worry about the hug, honey. It'll be fine," he said, then stopped again.

Suddenly he said, "It's okay, Helen. We have everything under control."

From somewhere in the hallway, a voice squeaked, "Yes, Mr. Van Hough."

"I'll call you if we need you."

"Yes sir, Mr. Van Hough," came the voice again and they could hear the sound of feet padding down the hallway.

"Thanks, Dad!" Victoria said as he glanced out the door and down the hall to make sure they were alone. "Sometimes she drives me crazy," she said.

"She's just doing her job. Unfortunately, her job often involves collecting intel for your mother," he said as he returned his attention to her suite, surveying the wreckage. "Wow! What happened here?"

"It's a little representative of my life. I'm cleaning out my closet and learning to take time to enjoy myself more."

"I'm so happy to hear that!" her father said and appeared to be beaming. "It's so important to have a good balance in your life. Unlike me, I'm heading to the office in a few minutes, but I wanted to let you know we were able to get your belongings off the plane." He reached out into the hall and returned with a laptop case. "We sent your clothes to the dry cleaner but I'm not optimistic they can be salvaged. I took your laptop to Sue, and she went over it to make sure it was in good shape. She got you a new case and transferred everything into it for you." Sue was the head of IT for Van Hough Industries and Victoria's best friend. She felt bad for not contacting her yesterday and telling her about the crash, but she wasn't up to reliving it again so soon. She made a mental note to call her today.

"Thanks, Dad," she said, taking the laptop bag and putting it on her bed. Her phone rang, and she picked it up and saw who was calling. It was Carter. "Sorry, Dad, I have to take this call." He looked at her phone and saw it was Carter, and Victoria noticed the wind being taken out of his sails. She leaned in, gave him a gentle hug and a sweet kiss on his cheek. He exited the room, closing the door behind him.

Victoria hesitated, took a deep breath, and answered the phone. "Hi, Carter."

"Hi, doll. Glad you are awake. How's your day going?"

"You know I don't want you to call me that. But my day is going well. I just saw my dad—"

Carter interrupted her in midsentence. "Sorry, Vicky," and the sound of a different name, especially that one, caused instant anger to well up in her.

"Carter—"

"I'm sorry," he interrupted with complete insincerity. "But listen, I need to make sure you know the plans for tonight."

The plans, as best as Victoria understood them, were to meet his parents for dinner. This would have been the first time she met them, and she wasn't up to the stress of the evening.

"Carter, I'm going to have to cancel for tonight. I'm just not up to it. Especially after the crash."

The silence on the other end made it very clear that Carter was unhappy to hear this. After a minute, he continued more sternly, "No, no! We've had these plans since before you left for South America. Canceling is not an option. We are not going to disappoint my parents like this."

"Carter, you realize I was in a serious accident on Thursday, right? I'm not feeling one hundred percent yet."

"Then I expect you to bring your eighty percent game and be ready at seven thirty when I pick you up. You said yourself, you escaped without a scratch."

"Carter—"

"Sorry, Vicky, I have another call I have to take. See you at seven thirty." Then the line went dead.

Victoria sat on her bed and put her phone down. She wondered what she was doing. Why was she continuing with this relationship? He was clearly not right for her. But every time she considered ending it with him, she heard her mother's voice. *He's a wonderful man, and he will keep you in the lifestyle you are accustomed to. And his parents are very well connected in our social circle.* All of which were correct. Except for the "wonderful man." He was actually an ass. Her dad was right. But breaking it off would be so troublesome with her mother. She knew this from experience. So she swallowed her pride and took the path of least resistance. She would be ready at seven thirty and would go on the date.

***

The ride to the restaurant was contentious. Carter wasn't happy, but Victoria had a feeling of self-satisfaction. As a silent protest, she wasn't ready until almost eight. Truthfully, her mother wasn't happy, either. She made it a point to send Helen up every ten minutes with offers to assist her with her preparations. As she was leaving, her mother showed her displeasure with her tardiness by pulling her to the side and saying, *Victoria, dear, a good woman doesn't make her man wait. You would be well advised to make sure to not let it happen again.* Victoria apologized, but it was less than half-hearted, which made Carter even more upset.

"I can't believe you are making my parents wait. This is not good," Carter complained as he pushed the accelerator of his Porsche to the point where it was clearly unsafe. Victoria knew it was best to not say anything more.

After twenty minutes of glorious silence, Carter wheeled up to the valet stand with a screech, sending Victoria lurching forward when it stopped. Carter removed the keys, got out, and slammed the door. He walked to the valet stand and threw his keys across the desk and they ricocheted around and onto the ground. Victoria got out of the car and met him at the curb. He turned, looked at Victoria, and his demeanor immediately changed. He smiled, took her hand, and they entered the restaurant. The instant change in his disposition concerned her greatly.

They walked, hand in hand, to the hostess station where they were greeted with a smile by a young woman with a name tag that read *Janet*. "Good evening, Mr. Jackson. Your parents are here already. Can I show you to your table?"

"Yes," Carter said through gritted teeth. The mention of his parents, who were already there, seemed to crack the veneer of his calm, controlled façade and he squeezed Victoria's hand more forcefully as they followed Janet to the table. As they weaved their way through the restaurant, Victoria took note of her surroundings. She was a very visual person and frequently cataloged what she saw. She noted the high-end furnishings, the large glass wine room with the exquisite selection of wines she enjoyed, and the delicious-looking crème brûlée being served at an adjacent table. Normally she looked forward to all these things, but tonight was different. She was uneasy around Carter, and the addition of his parents just made things worse.

As they arrived at the table, a distinguished-looking man of about sixty stood up, greeting Carter with a firm handshake.

"Hi, Dad. Sorry we're late. It took Victoria a little longer to get ready than we expected." Victoria saw how Carter had no problem throwing her under the proverbial bus, and

14

when he glanced back at her, she shot him daggers from her eyes.

With the mention of Victoria's name, Carter's father released his son's hand and unceremoniously swept him aside to have an unobstructed view of his new love interest.

"My, my, you are more lovely than I imagined," he said as a giant smile came over his face.

"Thank you, Mr. Jackson. That's nice of you to say," Victoria replied as she noticed she was looking down at him. He was a stocky man, and she had him by at least four inches. "Now I see where Carter gets his good looks," she said, exchanging pleasantries with him. He reached out his arms and moved close enough to her to provide an air-kiss on her cheek. He stepped back to his original place just in time. With the agility of a lynx, Carter's mother filled the gap between them, positioning herself well within Victoria's personal space. Victoria saw she was short as well, although this wasn't surprising for women since Victoria was nearly six feet tall. This evening she selected a nice pair of stilettos, adding nearly four more inches to her height advantage. Often this intimidated other women, but not her.

"It's not bad enough that your son is pawing the poor girl, but she has to deal with you, too?" her mother said, looking with contempt at both men.

"Oh, Elizabeth, I was only greeting the poor girl."

"Just sit down, Joseph, you are embarrassing yourself," she rebutted with an acidic tone. When he sat down as commanded, it was clear to Victoria who was boss of this household. "Now let me see you. Turn around darling," she said and made a twirling motion with her index finger. Victoria was well versed in this hand signal from her modeling days. She put her hand on her hip and did her best modeling turn, all the while feeling strange about these events. "Just lovely! I hope having my grandchildren doesn't ruin your shapely body. Make sure you have a good personal trainer. You want to keep in good shape for Carter. You know how men can stray!" she finished and waved her hand at the men. She walked over to her chair and looked down at it. "Isn't someone going to pull out my chair?" Both Carter and Joseph jumped up, but she again waved them off with disgust. "Oh, forget it! I'll get it myself," and she sat down with a huff.

Victoria pulled her own chair out as well since Carter had sat back down. She shot Carter a look as she pulled it under her, then instantly regretted it. She did not want to be someone like his mother.

They ordered drinks and appetizers, and the evening began with casual conversation. They discussed the weather, which had been unseasonably warm. Then they moved to politics. Carter's parents were quite involved in the last election cycle and expressed their approval that the current mayor was reelected. He was a close friend, and they enjoyed having friends in high places.

"You never know when you need a favor," said Joseph. "You scratch my back and I scratch yours," he said with a hearty laugh. "My checkbook gets a lot of things done."

"I'm sure your parents are the same way," Elizabeth said, looking at Victoria.

"I don't really pay attention to those things, to be honest. I know my parents host fundraisers at our estate, but I usually have other commitments."

"Oh my, you and Carter are our future. You need to be involved. Otherwise, who will look out for our interests? Our Carter is very active, aren't you, dear?" she said and looked at Carter. It made Victoria think of a child. She was treating him like a child, and it reminded her how her mother treats her. The thought annoyed her.

As the night progressed, she began to tune out the conversation. She nodded her head frequently and said "yes" often. It wasn't difficult since Carter's parents discussed themselves almost exclusively and talked about topics that interested them. The more they talked, the more Carter's mother reminded her of her own mother: self-absorbed, pretentious, and quite a miserable person. She emasculated her husband every opportunity she had. "Be quiet, Joseph, you don't know what you are talking about," was one of her favorite lines. "I bring you to pay the bill and be quiet," was another line she used. Victoria felt sorry for him, but she had seen many couples in her parents' social circles with the same dynamic. Her father, however, was different. He didn't let her mother get away with those kinds of attacks. But it wasn't for a lack of trying. Dad had a way about him where he could put her in her place. As she watched the interaction between the three family members, she realized Carter was far more like his mother than his father, and this concerned her. She vowed to never be chained to a relationship where she was forced to act like Carter's father. But she was already seeing the warning signs.

Victoria's Chateaubriand with béarnaise sauce arrived, and it caused her to reminisce about the many trips she and her father had taken to France. Of all the places they had traveled together, she loved France most. But her good feeling ended when Elizabeth changed the conversation.

"Carter tells me you work for your father?" said Elizabeth. The change surprised Victoria since they had been talking about her and Joseph for nearly an hour.

"Yes. I've worked for Van Hough Industries my entire life. But after getting my MBA from the Kellogg School of Management, they promoted me to vice president in charge of purchasing and procurement."

Elizabeth seemed unimpressed. She gave a "hmm" before returning her attention to her Wagyu beef. After savoring another bite, she replied, "My Carter graduated from Harvard Business School."

"Yes, I know. I was accepted there as well, but chose Northwestern instead," Victoria replied, with a subtle smugness that she hoped was nearly undetectable. She knew Northwestern's program ranked higher and enjoyed rubbing it in her face. Even if it was ever so slightly. When Elizabeth replied, "Indeed," Victoria swelled inside.

After a moment of silence, Elizabeth went on.

"You know, Victoria," she continued, "we have asked Carter to head up the development of a philanthropic organization for us. We have put a sizable amount of our fortune into it for Carter to donate on our behalf. We're really thrilled, aren't we, honey?"

Simultaneously, both Carter and Joseph responded, "Yes."

Elizabeth frowned and looked at Victoria. "Honestly, sometimes I feel like I'm in a bad Laurel and Hardy movie. Anyway, as I said, we are very excited. Do you go to charity events?"

"I'm afraid I don't. It's not my thing, but my parents are quite active and give frequently."

"Tsk, tsk," Elizabeth said while shaking her head and giving Victoria a look of disapproval. "If Carter ever decides to make you his wife, you will have to change that attitude. Perhaps you can start going with your parents."

Victoria had taken all she could handle for one night. She wiped her mouth and got up, walking around to Carter. She bent down and whispered in his ear, "I'm going to the ladies' room. When I get back, you are taking me home. And don't even think about blaming this on me. If you do, mommy dearest will hear all about how you paid your way through your last semester of school." With that, she spun around and headed to the ladies' room.

On returning to the table, she announced, "My apologies, Mr. and Mrs. Jackson, but I'm going to have to beg off of dessert. I'm not feeling like myself. I appear to still be suffering from the effects of the accident from two nights ago."

Joseph seemed surprised by her pronouncement, but Elizabeth wasn't. "Oh, that's right! I'm so sorry. We heard your father's plane was damaged beyond repair. Such a pity. I understand the cause was pilot error. I certainly hope your father wasn't flying at the time. That would make it awfully messy when dealing with the insurance company."

All Victoria could muster was, "Thank you and good

evening," as she spun around and walked toward the exit. She never turned around until she got to the valet stand, confident that Carter was following behind her, albeit at a safe distance.

CHAPTER THREE

Every muscle in her body ached. She couldn't understand why Josh was so tough on her, but she didn't mind. Victoria had woken up early since she had an appointment with her personal trainer. As she does four days a week, she met him in the workout room on the first floor of their expansive estate. Now, back in her suite, she stepped over to the full-length mirror and looked in. Even with her hair up in a towel and wearing shorts and a T-shirt, she still looked fabulous. She loved how her body looked and enjoyed putting in the effort to keep it that way. She turned her nose up to herself and sneered. "You'll have to keep your body toned for my son, Victoria," she said in a witchlike voice, trying to imitate Mrs. Jackson from last night. "I do it for myself, not your son," she said to her reflection, imagining it to be Carter's mother. She was an unpleasant shrew, and Victoria didn't care if she ever met her again. She walked over to her makeup table, took off the towel and began brushing her long, blond hair.

Victoria wasn't sure how it would end up, but the ride home was, mostly, uneventful. The only thing Carter said was, "You could have waited at least until we ate dessert. That was pretty selfish of you, you know." Of course

Victoria didn't dignify that ridiculous statement with a response. She was proud of herself for getting out of that horrible situation. It was clear that his mother was not going to let up. *Was she testing me?* Victoria thought for a second, then determined she didn't care. She wondered if Carter was having the same thoughts that she was about being near the end of their relationship. If he was, he didn't say so. She was sure she wouldn't hear from Carter for at least a day or so, if at all. That would be fine with her.

She opened a drawer, pulled out a blow-dryer, and began working on her mane. She thought about the information of Carter's college cheating that she dumped in his lap before they left the restaurant. The look on his face was one of sadness? Embarrassment? She wasn't sure, but for a minute she was disappointed that it had to come to that. She didn't want to hurt him.

Damn it. Why do I care about his feelings? He doesn't care about mine, she thought. But she cared. Not about him per se, but about hurting anyone's feelings. It wasn't something she enjoyed doing. It wasn't a part of her character, and her father didn't raise her that way. But he didn't raise her to be stepped on, either. She was just lucky she had that little piece of information. The Jacksons weren't the only ones with contacts who could uncover important or embarrassing information. In this case, her father brought this little morsel to her attention. His purpose was to open her eyes to his flawed character. Victoria knew it would come in handy some day and she was right. It's nice to have such a powerful trump card to play.

Knowing that work was piling up for her by the minute, she moved to her bed and picked up her new laptop case. She was thankful to have her friend Sue working with her. She was the best IT person she knew, and she had confidence that her laptop was in perfect working order. She opened the bag and removed it, raising the lid to boot it up. Victoria was surprised to find several handwritten Post-it Notes with handwriting that she knew well. They read:

Vic. I'm SO glad you are ok! I was so worried. Your computer is fine, but please take some time to relax. Life is too short. Love you. Sue.

She read them several times, and it brought a smile to her face. In one pocket of the bag, she found her charging cable with another Post-it Note.

You aren't listening. Stop what you are doing and relax.

Victoria laughed. In another pocket she found her mouse with, of course, another note.

Last chance! No turning back now, Vic!

She was persistent. She opened the last pocket and saw all the business cards and contact information she had collected on the trip before the plane crash. She fingered through them, reminding herself of each person associated with the information on the cards. The last one was her father's business card. "Strange. I have plenty of these. Don't need this one," she said as she attempted to flip it into the garbage can near her bed. Instead, it landed upside down on her night table and Victoria noticed the handwritten information on the back. She picked it up and examined it more closely. The name Nathaniel Robinson was written on it with a phone number below. Victoria thought but couldn't remember meeting this person. The information was written in her father's handwriting, so she held onto it and would give it back to him tomorrow.

She placed all the cards, with the last one on top, in a pile on her bedside table. She would need them as she worked on her notes from the trip. She sat on her bed, propped up by pillows, and began working on her laptop. She couldn't help but think the card had some significance, and after a few minutes, she picked it up again, this time noting it had a local area code. Why would someone from South America have a local area code? Then it hit her. This was the card her father gave her on the plane. The "nice" man recommended by him. She turned it over and over in her hands and a feeling of excitement formed in her stomach. She knew that any man recommended by her father was an outstanding person. But she also knew from experience that didn't guarantee a perfect match. Still, the possibility was more than she could resist. Victoria was a woman of great confidence and action. She remembered her father's words on the plane telling her he won't contact her. She would have to contact him if she wanted. "What have I got to lose?" she asked herself, following that up with, "Anything is better than Carter," and rolled her eyes. Besides, she had to get back to the new Victoria. The woman who lived for today. The one who took more time for herself and focused less on work. That was a lesson from the plane crash she didn't want to forget.

After taking her cell phone out, she opened it up and saved his phone number. She entered a contact title of *Blind Date Nate*, then composed a brief message.

Hi Nathaniel. My name is Victoria Van Hough. I know this is weird, but my father gave me your number and said you may be interested in talking or getting a cup of coffee. If so, let me know and we'll get something on our schedules. She pushed Send and imagined the possibilities. Victoria wanted to be with someone who would treat her with deep love, kindness, and respect. She wanted a partner in life. So far, all she had gotten were the Carters of the world. She refused to be someone's "arm candy." The thought of being a trophy wife made her want to vomit.

The knock on her door was loud and startled her out of her daydreaming of love and happiness. Behind the door, she heard Helen's voice. "Ms. Victoria, may I come in?"

"Yes, Helen." The door opened and the head of the household staff entered. As usual, she was dressed in a perfectly pressed uniform with her hair in a bun and conservatively made up.

"Ms. Victoria, I have a message from your mother. She would like for you to join her downstairs in the solarium for lunch."

Victoria's optimistic outlook that was forming just a few minutes ago crashed to the ground in a ball of flames. She knew her mother well and suspected she got wind of last night's disaster with Carter's parents. She would want to talk about it. No. She would want to lecture her about it and tell her about all the things she must change to be a good wife. She was definitely not up to hearing this.

"Please tell my mother that I'm not feeling up to it. I may see her for dinner instead," she said, knowing what was coming next.

"I'm afraid your mother is insisting that you attend, Ms. Victoria."

"Tell her I already have plans with my father," she responded, knowing it was a lie but that she could count on her father to keep up the ruse.

"Very well, ma'am," Helen said before exiting the room and closing the door. Victoria knew she would pay for that one, but she didn't care. Her spirits were lifted with the vibration of her phone indicating she had received a text. Excitedly, she picked it up and opened the message. It was from Blind Date Nate. *Hi Victoria. What an unexpected surprise! I would love to share coffee with you, although I'm a little intimidated by it. Coffee is your business after all, so I'll let you pick the place. How about Thursday night?*

Victoria opened up her calendar and confirmed that she was available. It was a date, and her spirits soared. "Carter who?" she said to herself. Life was definitely way too short. Unfortunately, Victoria would get a heartbreaking lesson in how short it actually was

CHAPTER FOUR

It only took four days for their date to come up on her calendar, but it seemed like an eternity to Victoria. This was the most demanding time of the year for Van Hough Industries, and Victoria was busier than ever. Despite her best efforts, her attempts to lead a better, more balanced life were not going well. All week, she arrived at the office early in the morning and didn't leave until well into the evening. Nevertheless, she guarded a one-hour spot on Thursday like she protected her collection of high-end handbags.

Thursday came, bringing with it a variety of meetings and conference calls that kept Victoria busy, and without lunch all day. As she closed her laptop for the evening, Paige, her assistant, apologized for bringing one last problem to her. There was an issue with customs on the west coast with one of their signature products. She was needed on the phone immediately. She had a thirty-minute drive to the coffee shop, so she took the call in her car on the way. As she pulled up along the curb in front of the coffee shop, she was still wrapping up her call. It took five more minutes making her late. As she exited her car, she was annoyed and tired, but knew she needed to re-center herself so she could be her best person with Nate. She knew first impressions were critical, and she wanted to nail this one.

As she reached the front door, she fished her phone out of her purse and turned it off. No one was going to interrupt her. If there were issues, she could address them when she finished. She took a deep, cleansing breath and pulled the door open. Her heart was racing and her palms were sweaty as she entered the café. Victoria was an adventurous person, so she insisted on making this a true, blind date. Although they exchanged a handful of texts leading up to the date, they did not talk about anything of substance and never sent photos. As a result, she had no idea what he looked like or what he would be wearing. Others would have been bothered by the mystery, but Victoria embraced it.

Being so tall, she could easily survey all the patrons and quickly zeroed in on a man sitting in a booth alone. Her heart skipped a beat as she realized he was quite a looker. She crossed her fingers and said, "Thanks, Dad," as she headed to the table.

On arrival to the table, she looked down at the gentleman, saying in an excited voice, "Hi! Are you Nathaniel?" He looked up, and she was taken by his deep green eyes.

"Oh, hi!" Nate said, standing up and inviting her to join him on the other side of the booth. She leaned in and gave him a hug. Victoria enjoyed physical touch and called herself a hugger. She took a breath of his cologne. It wasn't a scent she knew, but it was wonderful. She sat down and got settled in, but found it difficult to take her eyes off him. Those eyes, and his dark brown, curly hair, just long enough to be stylish, but not too long made him quite attractive. They would make beautiful babies together, she thought.

"You are Nathaniel, right?" she asked again, not getting an answer the first time. "Because it would be really embarrassing if I just sat down with some other total stranger." She flashed him a big smile.

"I'm so sorry. Yes. Of course. I'm Nathaniel Robinson,

but please call me Nate. It's so nice to meet you. I have to be honest, Victoria. You are stunningly beautiful."

Victoria never tired of hearing that and demurred at his comment, giving him a bashful "Thank you" and a brief touch of his hand, which was soft and warm. "I have to admit, I know nothing about you. My father just gave me your number and said if I wanted to meet a super guy, to call you. So I did."

"Wow. That is a ringing endorsement from a man who I admire so much. He's a big part of how I got to where I am today."

"Really? I'd love to hear about it," Victoria inquired.

"I met your dad when I was in my junior year of undergrad studies. I was giving a speech about congenital heart defects that he attended. He approached me afterwards and told me how impressed he was. He wanted to know more. We met several times after and he encouraged me to pursue becoming a doctor." Up till now, Victoria hadn't really paid any attention to the clothes he was wearing, but now saw he was in green surgical hospital scrubs. This made sense now. Nate continued, "He hooked me up with an amazing mentor, and together, they changed my life. They helped me get into research projects to strengthen my chances of getting into med school. They helped me with my admission essay and prepared me for the interview. I would never have been able to get to this point without him."

As she listened to his story, Victoria was filled with pride. This was just another example of the greatness of her father. He changed people's lives, and she loved that about him.

"That definitely sounds like my dad. He's a pretty amazing guy. So where are you in the school process now? I see you are wearing your sexy scrubs," she said, giving him a wink.

"I'm finishing up the last year of my surgical residency and have applied for my pediatric surgical residency. Hopefully, I get in. That's really where my passion lies."

"You want to operate on children?"

"Absolutely. I have a congenital heart defect and although I was too young to remember going through surgeries, I had several of them. Those doctors saved my life, so I want to pay it forward and give some other child a chance to live. I know it sounds a little cheesy, but it's how I feel."

Her heart was melting, listening to him pour himself out for her. So much compassion. So much dedication. "Oh my God, Nate. It's not cheesy at all. It's amazing."

The moment was interrupted by the server who had been patiently waiting to take their order for several minutes. This was her third trip to the table, and they would not deny her this time. "Can I get you something to eat or drink?" she said with a slightly irritated voice.

Nate pointed to Victoria. "You are the expert here. What do you suggest?"

Victoria laughed. "You aren't going to get our products here, silly. We'll just take two coffees for now." Having succeeded at getting something out of the occupants of booth twelve, she whisked away to attend to other business.

"I feel like I'm at a disadvantage here. You know my father and the company and I know so little about you."

"Actually, one of the things that impressed me about your father is that he didn't go on and on about his business, or its success. It was all about helping me. So other than knowing it's an importer, I really have very little else."

"My father started by importing high-end coffees and teas. He realized there was a market for these products and that people would pay a premium for them. That was over twenty years ago. Now we import whiskey, brandy, nuts, rum, wine, and a lot of other products. I'm in charge of purchasing so my father and I go all over the world looking for quality products to buy. It's an amazing company and I love working there. It keeps me very busy, but I'm working hard to have a better work-life balance."

Their coffee arrived and Victoria looked it over like a

gemologist would examine a new diamond. She held the cup up to her nose and took a deep breath. After putting the cup back down, she used her hands to circle her throat while making a quiet choking sound. This caused them both to break out into laughter. She loved having fun, and a wonderful sense of humor was an essential part of the character of her partner. The fact that Nate was laughing was a good sign.

Nate spent some of their time telling her about a few of the more difficult surgeries he had done during his residency. Victoria listened attentively, although a few of the details made her stomach do flips. Luckily they were only enjoying coffee and not a meal since this was not pleasant dinner conversation. She shared stories of her last trip to South America, although she intentionally stayed away from telling him about the plane crash. She didn't feel it was appropriate to share that detail right now. Maybe another time.

Their conversation flowed naturally with each person telling about themselves, then listening as the other took a turn. Victoria felt so comfortable with him. All the challenges in her life seemed to disappear with the sound of his voice.

"So, tell me about—" Nate stopped talking mid-sentence. A frown came across his face as he reached into his pocket and pulled out a cell phone. Victoria could tell it was vibrating. "Hello. Yes. Oh, no. I'll be there in fifteen minutes. Bye." He looked at Victoria with a face full of disappointment that was obvious despite his best efforts. "I'm sorry, Victoria. I have to go. There is an emergency surgery and I need to be there." He stood up and pulled out his money clip, peeled off a twenty-dollar bill, and placed it on the table. "Can we do this again?" he asked and flashed a vibrant smile that made Victoria smile back.

"Absolutely! Text me."

As he walked away, it was Victoria's turn to be disappointed. She wanted to spend more time getting to know him. So articulate, so intelligent, and so damn handsome. Why hadn't someone like him come into her life before? She took a drink of her coffee and had to force it down. "Oh, crap. That is so awful." She sat back in the booth and took a deep breath. She could still smell the faint scent of his goodness. She closed her eyes and began imagining the possibilities. Out of habit, she reached into her purse, retrieved her phone, and turned it back on. It immediately vibrated, indicating she had a voice mail. She realized her mistake when it vibrated again. A pit formed in her stomach as she listened to the first voice mail. It was from Carter.

"Hi, Vickie." She cringed. "I know we had a rough time the other night with my parents. But I know you were under a little stress and I forgive you. How could I not? Let's get together this weekend. Call me."

Victoria rolled her eyes as she pressed the Delete button. She didn't apologize and had no intentions of doing so. His mother was rude, and she couldn't believe he never stepped in to defend her. She pressed Play on the second voice mail.

"Hi, Vickie. It's me. I just called in a favor and got tickets to the play I want to see. Call me and I'll give you the details."

"Unbelievable," she said, shaking her head in disbelief. Her hope that Carter shared her feelings of their relationship's demise was dashed. *I guess I'm going to have to take things into my own hands with this*, Victoria thought. But before she could, Victoria had to figure out how to manage her mother, which was no small feat.

***

Even the dilemma of how to delicately end things with Carter given their families' connection couldn't dampen Victoria's spirits. She was walking on air as she glided into the main house from the underground garage complex where she'd parked her Mercedes. She hurried down the series of hallways to the sweeping marble staircase leading to the main floor. Victoria had dodged her mother for several days now, and she was hoping to keep that trend intact. At the top of the stairs, she had just a left turn and a long walk to the back stairs leading to her suite and freedom. A few steps down the hallway, she slowed, turned her head around, and looked behind her. Nothing. As her head snapped forward, she ran right into Helen, who seemed to have appeared out of thin air. The force of the collision knocked Helen backwards into the nearby doorframe, and she grasped the air for something to keep from falling to the ground.

"Oh my gosh, Helen!" Victoria said as she reached out and grabbed Helen's arm to help steady her. "I'm so sorry. I didn't see you. Are you alright?"

"Yes, I'm fine," she said as she stood up and smoothed out her uniform. "I'm glad to have run into you, Ms. Victoria. Not literally, of course." They both laughed uneasily. Victoria knew what was coming next, and she wasn't disappointed. "I just left your mother in the kitchen and she would appreciate an audience with you before bedtime. I can't stress how important it is for you to speak with her."

Victoria let out a deep sigh. "I'll go now. Thanks." She turned around, heading back down the hallway toward a conversation that would not end well. Just before reaching the kitchen, she turned to look behind her. Helen was gone. "She's a damn ghost," she said to herself and turned her head forward just in time to see her mother. Luckily, she was able to stop before crashing into her, but the fear of contact caused her mother to spill the cup of tea she was carrying.

"Oh, dear!" her mother exclaimed. She had closed her eyes in anticipation of the contact with her daughter and had reopened them when it didn't happen. "Victoria! You need to be more careful and watch where you are going! I could have been hurt! You caused me to spill my tea."

Out of nowhere, Helen appeared with a towel. "I'll get that, ma'am."

All the commotion made Victoria's head spin. She wondered how she could run into two people in a twenty-thousand-square-foot house.

"Thank you, Helen," she said, then turned her attention to her daughter. "Come with me, my dear, you and I need to talk." Alice spun around and plodded back into the kitchen, taking a seat on a stool in front of a large prep table in the center of the room. The room was enormous, with restaurant-style commercial appliances used by the staff to prepare the meals. Including Helen, the staff usually numbered six, although her mother occasionally took her wrath out on one a year, leaving an opening to be filled by the next unsuspecting victim. Helen was the exception. She had been with the family for as long as Victoria could remember. She reached under the table and pulled out another stool, choosing to sit across from, rather than next to her.

"How was your evening, dear? Were you working late again?"

Her mother always beat around the bush. Victoria found it to be rather tedious and annoying. "Mother, it's late. Can't we just get to the point of this conversation? I'm tired."

"As you wish," Alice said as she removed her glasses and placed them on the table in a dramatic gesture, adding to the seriousness of this conversation. Her mother had been a theater major in college and loved to add drama whenever possible. "I heard some very disturbing news about your evening with the Jacksons the other night."

"Interesting. And where did you hear this from?" she asked, knowing her mother normally didn't give up her sources.

"Actually, Helen heard it from some staff at the Jackson house. Apparently Mrs. Jackson was quite upset, so I'm told."

A vision entered Victoria's mind of all the staff members

from the various wealthy households having meetings to complain about their employers, causing Victoria to laugh out loud.

"I'm not sure laughing is an appropriate response, Victoria," her mother said with a sneer. "This is a serious matter."

"What serious matter are we discussing?" His voice carried into the kitchen before his appearance, but Victoria recognized her father and was thrilled to see him enter.

"It's really not your concern, James. This is between the two of us," Alice insisted, pointing a bony finger at Victoria and then back at herself to emphasize the exclusivity of their club.

"Mother was just telling me about the staff member rumor network. Apparently, they share ugly stories about their employers," Victoria said with renewed confidence now that her father was there to support her position.

"Do you suppose we will make their next newsletter?" Jim blurted out, and they both broke into a laughing fit.

Alice exploded, slamming her fist on the stainless-steel table, causing the dishes to rattle. "This is not a game! Victoria was very ill-mannered to a member of our social circle! These things get around and I will not have it."

"Were you 'ill-mannered,' Victoria?" her father asked, using air quotes around the word "ill-mannered" as a way to press his wife's buttons, then winking.

"How can I put this? The woman is a troll and would eat her own young except that Carter isn't a fit meal for even a troll."

Victoria and her father laughed again with Jim saying, "It's actually an excellent description of her. She's quite disagreeable."

"Stop it right now, you two! Shame on you James for encouraging your daughter to act this way. You could be talking about her future husband and mother-in-law."

"Not likely, Alice. I read in the staff newsletter that our daughter has her eyes on a hot young surgeon," Jim said, and burst out laughing. Victoria laughed, but uncomfortably so. She was shocked to hear that her father knew about her date so soon and that he would expose the information to her mother. Alice would definitely file that away for another discussion. For a time when her father was not around to come to her defense. But Victoria took advantage of the situation in order to make her exit.

"I would love to stay and continue this conversation, but it's been a long day and I need to be in the office early tomorrow. Good night," Victoria said before whirling around and leaving the room. With no one in her way this time, she retreated to her suite, leaving behind angry voices that got louder and louder as she sped up toward her sanctuary. She was so thankful her father came when he did. She would be so lost without him.

CHAPTER FIVE

A playful nature was something that Victoria had in abundance. She loved practical jokes, puzzles, and other fun things that added interest to life. Unfortunately, most of the stuffed shirts she had dated so far in her life have not appreciated that aspect of her personality. *Victoria, society expects us to act a certain way and when we don't we risk losing our standing,* they would say in one way or another. She mocked them by using a stuffy old man's voice.

She and Nate had occupied their time apart with text messages and phone conversations, sharing lots of interesting and fun things about each other. They talked about foods they liked: pizza for him and sushi for her. Nate was a baseball guy, and Victoria was into opera. But they agreed to embrace their differences and learn from each other. Nate said she would look so cute in a baseball cap, and vowed to buy her one at their first game. They planned to meet today, and Victoria couldn't wait to see him again. But he was very evasive about where and wouldn't share any details regarding their activities. She wasn't worried. Nate had a good heart and a wonderful sense of humor. So she played along, knowing that he was the prize at the end of the game.

He had texted the first and only instructions to her that morning: *Welcome to my world, where there is joy everywhere. Sometimes you see it, sometimes you bring it, and sometimes you are it. Go to University Hospital. Arrive promptly at 10am. Introduce yourself at the front desk.* She parked in the garage and walked to the front entrance. Her heart was racing, and the chance to see Nate again filled her with excitement. Since her destination was a hospital, she wasn't sure how to dress, so she erred on the more conservative side. She selected a solid yellow knee-length dress with a few of her favorite jewelry pieces and a pair of flats. It was important for her to look good, and she was sure she accomplished that and then some. She entered the hospital and walked into the two-story glass atrium up to the front desk. The entry looked more like a high-end hotel than a hospital, and it impressed Victoria. With an electric smile, she greeted the attendants.

"Hi! My name is Victoria. I was told to come here and there would be further instructions."

The elderly man behind the desk didn't seem to know what she was talking about, and Victoria had a moment of concern. He turned to another woman at the desk and they whispered among themselves. The woman came over and said, "Hi, Victoria. Someone left these things for you." She reached under the desk and produced an envelope and handed it to her. She reached back under and produced a single red rose and gave her that as well. Then, she leaned over the top of the desk as if she had some secret to tell her, so Victoria leaned in to listen. "I probably don't have to tell you, but he is really a special person. I hope you enjoy your day."

Victoria was touched by her sentiment. She thanked the woman and took a seat on a nearby couch. The rose was beautiful, and she filled her nose with its scent. After placing the rose across her lap, she took the envelope and opened it. Inside, she found a voucher for the cafeteria, a hospital map, a note, and another envelope. The note said: *Follow your nose. It will know where to go. Use the voucher and buy some goodies. Stop at the next spot marked on the map and open the next envelope.* Victoria was enjoying the quest, but couldn't wait to see Nate, so she collected up all the pieces and headed off, following the signs and her nose to the cafeteria.

Buy some goodies, huh? She looked around and thought, *What would bring joy?* She walked around and surveyed the items available. Everything was prepackaged and definitely didn't say joy. At one end, there was a door leading to an outdoor eating area. When she went outside, she saw a bake sale raising money for an organization that helped sick kids. *Jackpot!* She couldn't use the voucher, so she surmised that this was not part of Nate's original plan, but that was okay. She was improvising. Besides, nothing said joy more than cookies, brownies, and rice crispy treats! She paid for the treats, gathered everything else up, and left the cafeteria area. She found a nearby bench and sat down to organize her items. She folded the original note with the vouchers and put it in the bag of goodies. *They may end up in a scrapbook someday,* she thought. She opened the second smaller envelope, which was inside the first, and saw it contained another note, which she quickly opened. It read: *Go down the hall in front of you, take the elevator to the fourth floor and report to the nurse's station. Before you get there, make sure you tune up. Tune up?* she thought. Victoria was a lot of things, but a competent singer was not one of them. The shower walls were the only things to ever hear her singing voice, and she intended to keep it that way. Regardless, she would play along and continue the quest. After reorienting herself using the map Nate provided, she easily found the elevator, stepped on, and rode it to the fourth floor. When the doors opened, she saw a sign on the wall that read *Pediatric Oncology.* Her heart sank. She wasn't well versed in hospitals, but she knew this was a place where they treated children with cancer. She looked around, wondering if she got off on the wrong floor. After reviewing the instructions, she was convinced this was the right spot. But this quest was about joy. How could joy end on a floor where little innocent children were being treated for such a horrible disease? Uncertain, she proceeded to the nurse's station, trusting that Nate had something special in store.

She walked up to the person behind the desk and said, "Hi! I'm Victoria. I was told to come here, but I have no idea why. Can you help me?"

A huge smile came over her face and Victoria knew she was in the right place. "Hi, Victoria! You are definitely in the right place. Hang out here for a minute." She pulled a phone out of her pocket and typed in a message. Within minutes, people began gathering. She came around into the hallway where the others were. "My name is Janice. Nate said he suggested having your singing voice ready, right?" Victoria nodded, but the lump in her throat prevented her from saying anything.

Janice faced the assembled staff members and said, "Ready?" On command they began singing:

Ooh, ooh ooh ooh oo-ooh ooh oo-ooh . . . don't worry . . . ooh ooh ooh ooh oo-ooh ooh oo-ooh . . . be happy.

Two male staff members sang, and Victoria immediately recognized the song. It made her happy. Or should she say, full of joy!

As the group sang the chorus, Janice took Victoria's hand and led her down the hall, the strolling minstrels following close behind. They got to a conference room and Janice opened the door, allowing Victoria to enter first. She couldn't believe her eyes. At the tables and sitting on the couches was a group of young children. Many of them had no hair, some of them were connected to IV poles, but they all had enormous smiles on their faces and all of them were now singing along with the staff. They all happily sang at the top of their voices.

Victoria couldn't believe what she was seeing. In the middle of utterly devastating health problems, there was joy everywhere. She looked, and in the back of the room she spotted Nate. He was smiling ear to ear, and a tear rolled down Victoria's cheek. As they finished the song, she looked around. There were signs greeting her with big hearts drawn on them. She circled the room, clapping and high-fiving every child. When they finished, everyone clapped and cheered. Nate stood up and thanked everyone for helping.

"You guys were great! Thanks so much!" he said as he got to the door. He closed it and turned his attention to Victoria. She jumped into his arms and all the children let out a tremendous cheer. Then the chanting started.

"We want snacks! We want snacks!" After two choruses, it dawned on Victoria that they were chanting at her. She raised the two bags of goodies she had in her hands and the kids cheered.

Nate took the bags and unloaded them on the conference room table. He looked at Victoria and told her, "You did amazing." She remembered his first note and realized she saw joy, brought joy, and was joy.

"Nate, I'm blown away. I had no idea."

"Come on. Let's meet the kids."

***

As they exited the hospital for the short walk to their next destination, Victoria was floating on clouds. She and Nate strolled hand in hand, and she reflected on the day so far. She sat with each child and played games, colored pictures, or assembled a puzzle as they told her their story. The strength and resolve she saw in them frequently brought tears to her eyes, and many of the children reached out to hold her hand and comfort her. How was this possible? she thought. Children who were engaged in the battle of their lives were consoling her. Just the thought of those brave souls caused her eyes to mist up. Nate looked over at her as they walked and saw a small tear roll down her cheek. He stopped and lovingly wiped it away and Victoria looked away, feeling slightly shameful at her display of uncontrolled emotion. They began walking again and Nate spoke.

"I know how you are feeling, Victoria. You are so conflicted inside with so many emotions. You are angry that these innocent children are suffering. You are amazed by their resolve and courage. You may even feel a little guilt. I felt the same way the first time I met some of these children. In fact, I still do."

It took Victoria by surprise how accurately he summarized her feelings, and she squeezed his hand harder to express how thankful she was that he understood.

"It doesn't get any easier. But the more you see them, the more you want to help. That's why I'm so dedicated to this path I'm on. So laser-focused on getting into my pediatric surgical residency program. Victoria, a surgeon changed my life and I want to be that same life changer for other children."

Hearing him so eloquently express his hopes and dreams gave Victoria a deeper understanding of Nate and a greater appreciation of him and his journey. It sounded like a journey she would love to take with him. She could be his partner and he hers.

"What are the next steps for you?" she asked as they turned a corner and across another grass field.

"I have completed the application process for Duke and Stanford, and I'm waiting to hear from them. It could be any day now. I pray every day that one of them says yes."

Victoria nodded, showing her understanding, but the information surprised her. Since their relationship was so new, she hadn't given it any thought, but now the possibility of them being separated was very real and it sent a pain to her stomach. "What if neither one accepts you? Will you just stay here and do adult surgery?" She hoped her words didn't give away her feelings, but that was exactly the outcome she would prefer. She felt guilty having those thoughts and hoped she didn't come off to him as selfish.

"Oh, no. I will never give up on my dream. I'm so close I can almost feel it." Victoria sensed a level of determination in him she hadn't seen in most people. "Have you ever wanted something so bad?" he asked. "Something that you think about every day and every night? Something that drives you when you feel spent and have nothing else to give?" He looked at her, focusing on her eyes. "That's where I am now. It's going to happen."

"I completely understand where you are coming from, Nate, and I love that you are so dedicated to making it happen."

"Honestly, my biggest challenge right now is financial. As you can imagine, all this schooling and not being able to earn a salary has taken a huge financial toll on me. I haven't actually sat down and created a spreadsheet. It scares me to even think about it, but it will take many years before I see any light at the end of that tunnel. I'm not doing it for the money, but it's an unfortunate reality that I will have to deal with sooner, rather than later." He looked over at Victoria and said, "But finances shouldn't be a topic of discussion so early in a relationship. I'm sorry I brought it up. But I feel so comfortable with you."

She smiled back at him. "You can talk to me about anything." And she meant it, although the thought of relocation and financial hardship were troubling topics for her and their fledgling relationship. Her mother would never accept that she could be involved in a long-distance relationship, and she would definitely reject someone who was in financial ruin; even if it was temporary and even if he became a successful surgeon. Her only hope of making that work was through her father. He had a strong connection to Nate and was intimately familiar with his character. She would have to join forces with him to beat back any objections from her mother. It would be a tall order, but she was hopeful they could make it happen.

"We're here," Nate said as they walked up to the front of the building. He opened the door, and they entered. The door slammed closed behind them, leaving a cacophonous sound that echoed throughout the aluminum skin and steel structure. Voices could be heard in the distance, along with intermittent whistles. There was some kind of sports activity going on here, but Victoria wasn't sure what. Sports was not something she paid any attention to in her life. She never went to baseball games or watched football on the television. Not that she was opposed to the idea of sports after all; she watched the Olympics occasionally and marveled at the skills of the participants. In fact, her father flew her to Sochi, where she attended several event finals while her father negotiated a lucrative contract to import Russian vodka. But mostly her family spent their time attending plays and going to the opera. Victoria couldn't name a single player on a professional baseball team, but if American soprano Renée Fleming or German tenor Jonas Kaufmann walked by, she would know them immediately.

They walked from the front entrance across the main lobby to the doors leading to the skating rink, which, apparently, was their destination. Nate suggested Victoria wait while he had a word with the security person at the door. They appeared to exchange pleasantries, each nodding while the other talked. After a minute, they shook hands and Nate waved Victoria to join him. He opened the door and followed her through.

She walked up to the glass and looked onto the ice. Victoria was tall at six feet, but the men on the ice seemed much taller. As she watched, the activity on the ice fascinated her. Ten men chased a black piece of rubber around. Some men left the surface as others came on. It reminded her of a carefully choreographed ballet performance. She watched the black rubber skitter to a stop in the corner near her. Three of the players violently crashed into the wall, causing the glass to shake and wave from the collision. The action made Victoria jump back in surprise. She heard laughing behind her and turned to see Nate walking toward her with a pair of ice skates slung over each shoulder.

"Why did you jump?" he asked, still laughing between words, then taking her by the shoulder and pretending to imitate the action on the ice. She was immediately aware of his hands on her and she enjoyed his touch. But Victoria had a deep, playful streak in her. In an instant, she grabbed his hands, spun him around, and pinned him against the plexiglass barrier, leaning the weight of her body onto his.

"Now who's laughing?" Victoria said, leaning in close to his face. She could smell his cologne. He smelled so good.

Nate leaned in and whispered in her ear, "That was kind of hot. Can we do it again?"

They both laughed as Victoria backed up, releasing Nate. She gave him a playful wink.

"So what's next?" she inquired. "Surely we won't be skating with these beasts."

"Absolutely not. Based on what you just showed me, I would be fearful of their safety," Nate said and winked back at her.

A whistle blew a long blast, a loud horn sounded, and the ice suddenly cleared of activity. Victoria watched as a machine came onto the ice and began clearing off the shavings leaving beautiful, clean ice in its wake. "I assume we are going out there?" she said as Nate led her to a bench and they sat down.

"Of course. Have you ever been ice-skating before?" he asked as he positioned himself on his knees in front of Victoria.

"Never."

He removed her first shoe, slid a skate onto her foot, and began lacing it up as he said, "Hopefully you have good health insurance." She impishly swatted him on the shoulder. He put on her other skate before sitting next to her and putting on his own. He stood up just as the ice machine left the rink and the doors closed behind it. Nate held out his hand and encouraged her to stand up. "This is the straightforward part," he said as he helped her onto her skates. Her ankles were completely unprepared for this new balancing act and she felt awkward, standing on the blades.

"You can do it," he said, and she liked the confidence he

was showing in her. He was very reassuring. She took a tentative step forward, then another. After taking her hand, he slowly led her to the door that opened onto the ice surface.

"Show me what you have," she said teasingly as they got to the ice. He stepped on, pushed off, and glided ten feet away, demonstrating his high skill level. "Hey! You have done this before! No fair." He flashed her a smile as he gracefully glided back to her, holding out his hand, encouraging her to step on the ice.

"Go slow. I'll be here, don't worry."

She put one foot on, then the other as he took her hands in his. With a gentle tug, he pulled her along. Victoria was thankful for her high level of self-confidence. Anyone else would have experienced a crisis considering all the bobbing and jerking she was doing to help maintain her balance. It was fun, but not very ladylike, and she wondered what Nate was thinking. She looked up from the ice where her eyes had been locked and saw that he was laser-focused on her. He was so attentive and supportive.

"Great job, Victoria. Now use your foot to push off." He demonstrated, and she followed his lead. "Now use the other foot, too." As she used her legs to create her own forward motion, she noticed Nate was barely holding her hands. He released his grip, and she glided under her own power. Just as she was feeling more confident, she lost her balance and began the bobbing and jerking motions over again. Until now, she was focused solely on her and Nate when, out of the corner of her eye, a compact bundle of energy flashed by her, causing her to lose her balance again. When she looked up, she realized that several other people had joined them in the rink, skating around the oval surface at various speeds and exhibiting different skill levels. Seeing all the people gave Victoria encouragement, and she used her legs more to build forward momentum. Faster and faster she went until a realization hit her. She looked up at Nate, who was skating backwards but in front of her, and yelled, "How do I stop?" Nate slowed down to catch her, but her energy carried her into his chest. Their feet became entangled and down they went. Nate fell on his rear end as Victoria then landed on top of him. Together they skidded to a stop.

"Oh my God, Nate! Are you okay? I'm so sorry!" She was still on top of him and looking right into his eyes. Deep green and beautiful.

"I'm fine. Really." She was glad to hear that, but not in any particular hurry to get off him. She liked the closeness they were experiencing and noticed how easy it would have been to lean in and steal a kiss. The world faded away as she stared into his eyes.

The shrill sound of a whistle shattered their moment. They looked up and saw a teenage boy with *Guard* on his shirt leaning over them with his hands on his knees. Just for effect, he blew the whistle again and startled them. "Let's go, you two. Move it along!"

They all laughed as Victoria rolled off him. Nate got to his feet and helped Victoria do the same. "I guess I should have taught you how to stop first," Nate said sheepishly. He took Victoria by the hand and they worked together to make several more laps around the ice rink before exiting and taking a seat together.

She pulled her phone out of her pocket and unlocked the screen. "I'm sorry, Nate. It's our busy time of the year and I need to check for any messages."

"No worries," he reassured her. "I completely understand."

She checked her text messages and saw there were two from Carter. She didn't bother reading them, but just the sight of them brought her mood down significantly. She also had two voice mails: one from work and one from Carter. She listened to the work message, but not the one from Carter. It was an urgent request to call the office about a shipment that might be delayed.

"Damn. I'm sorry, Nate. I have to go. Work is calling me

about a problem."

He helped her take the skates off and get to her feet. She loved that he was so understanding. Getting control of her life would have to wait a bit. Work was busy, and they needed her. Her father needed her. She knew there would be limits to Nate's understanding, but she wasn't even close yet, and before she got there, she would have everything under control in her life. Victoria didn't understand that her life was about to be turned upside down.

CHAPTER SIX

On the ride home, Victoria made several work calls and when she hung up with the last one, she said, "Crisis averted. For now." She was pleased with her accomplishment and it raised her spirits. She finally had a chance to reflect on her time with Nate. She still couldn't believe what a wonderful man he was, so patient and loving. She was so impressed by his dedication and thought he could make an excellent partner. The thing she liked most was how willing he was to expose his feelings to her. Victoria was more guarded with her deepest thoughts, but seeing him at his most vulnerable gave her hope that she could open up, too. She was starting to believe this could be the real deal. Victoria saw the way he looked at her, how he protected her and how he touched her, and was sure he felt the same way.

She was tingling all over as she pressed the button to open the gate to their compound. Once open, she proceeded down the driveway and into the underground garage, parking next to her mother's Bentley. She saw her father's spot was unoccupied. "Great. Just me and Mother. Can't wait."

She exited the car, headed into the house, and up the

stairs to the main floor. She made a right at the top of the stairs and cut through the family room, heading to the kitchen for something to drink before going to bed. She was nearly to the end of the room when she heard a voice. The only voice she didn't want to hear.

"Victoria, dear. Can I have a word with you?" It was her mother, and she cringed at the sound of her voice. Whenever she got ambushed by her, it was never a good thing.

"Mother, I'm tired. Can we do this another day?"

"I'm afraid not, dear. Come have a seat by me. Let's talk," she said, patting the seat next to her by the fireplace. Obediently, she moved to the chair and sat down.

"What is so important that it can't wait until tomorrow?"

"Don't take that tone with me, Victoria. I'm your mother and I will have respect."

This comment made Victoria angry. Although she was raised to have complete respect for her parents, her mother used that to push her around, and she resented it. But she kept her comments to herself. Hopefully, this would also help speed the conversation along and she could move on.

"How are things going with you lately, dear?" This opening line was typical for her mother. She usually started the conversation off with idle chitchat before going for the kill.

"Fine, Mother. How about you?" Victoria said, playing along and giving a big, contrived smile.

"Oh, sweetie. You don't seem like yourself lately. You have been distant, and I missed you at lunch today. Were you at the office?"

Her mother was president of the company and knew if she was there or not. "I'm an adult, Mother. I have a life."

"Of course you do, dear. But you are so very young. I want to keep you from making a mistake," she said as she reached over to the coffee table and retrieved her cup of tea. She took a sip and said, "So how is Carter these days?"

"Speaking of mistakes," Victoria mumbled under her

breath.

"I'm sorry. I didn't hear you, dear. You need to enunciate your words better." She paused for effect, knowing full well what Victoria had said. "I've been told by a reliable source that you haven't been taking Carter's calls or answering his text messages. What is going on?"

Victoria knew it wouldn't do any good to try to explain herself. Her mother had handpicked Carter, and she was convinced that he would make the perfect husband.

"I've been busy, Mother. You know we are in the middle of our busiest time of the year."

"Yes, of course, dear. But let me give you some advice. You have to make yourself available for a man. I have everything under control at work, so there is no excuse. Time is passing you by and it's time to settle down, get married and have children." She took another sip of tea before continuing, "Carter is in a very important position with his father's company and he can more than adequately support you in our current lifestyle. Besides, he and his family are very active in our community, so it would not look good for me if you didn't follow through on our commitment."

"Our commitment? Mother, this is your commitment."

"A family commitment is meant to be kept by all members. We have to stick together to ensure the continuation of our family's name and reputation."

"Mother, I'll try to call him in the next day or so. That's the best I can do." Victoria wasn't lying. She had every intention of calling him, but not for the purpose her mother thought.

"I'm afraid that won't do, Victoria. I anticipated that response and took matters into my own hands." She directed her comment toward the hallway and said, "Please join us." There was the sound of footsteps and out of the darkness appeared Carter. He walked over to Victoria and stood before her.

"Hi, Victoria. Nice to see you again."

She looked over at her mother, and saw the smug satisfaction on her face. Victoria turned back to see Carter getting down on one knee and taking her hands. It horrified her. All she could do was repeat to herself, Please don't propose, please don't propose.

"From the first time I met you, I knew you were supposed to be mine. You are beautiful and the perfect complement to me to make beautiful babies." He looked over at her mother. "How could we let this fabulous woman down? She deserves grandkids." Her mother feigned embarrassment and waved a hand toward him. "I'm not sure what I've done to make you want to push me away, but I'm willing to change. We are perfect together. Please don't ignore me."

Having seen enough to know the train was back on the track, her mother cleared her throat, causing a pause in the action that Victoria was thankful for. "Thank you for coming over, Carter. I'll leave you two lovebirds alone." She stood up and walked out of the room.

"Victoria, don't make me grovel for your love." He stood up and pulled gently on her to encourage her to stand. She did, and he led her over to an enormous sectional sofa. He sat down and rubbed the cushion next to him. "Please join me."

Victoria walked to the door, glancing down the hall both ways to ensure they were alone, then returned to stand in front of Carter. She looked at Carter and said, "This isn't going to happen."

Carter first looked surprised, then crushed. "Victoria, what's wrong?"

She extended her hands, and when he took them, she encouraged him to get to his feet. She led him out of the room and down the hallway. As they reached the front door, she turned to face him. "This is my mother's plan, Carter, not mine. You need to leave."

"Victoria . . ." Carter said, but before he could finish, she opened the door and whooshed him out, closing it behind him. As she walked away, she felt a twinge of sadness for Carter. It was apparent that her mother had manipulated him and set up the encounter herself. She resolved to address the whole thing with her mother.

CHAPTER SEVEN

"Hi, Ms. Van Hough?" The sound of Paige's voice over the intercom caused Victoria to jump. She was so involved in her work that she had blocked the rest of the world out. "I'm sorry to bother you."

"It's okay, Paige. What do you need?"

"Mr. Van Hough would like to see you in his office before you leave."

"Okay. Thanks," she replied, and the voice emanating from the speaker on her desk phone disappeared. It was a busy time for Van Hough Industries, so she knew her father wanted to go over some last-minute instructions before he left for a work trip to Denver this evening. He always copied her on his itinerary, so she remembered his plane would be leaving in two hours. He was undoubtedly planning on doing the flying himself. She retrieved a notepad and a pen from her desk and headed to her father's office down the hall. While walking, she reviewed in her head the upcoming priorities for the company, anticipating the topics they would discuss. At the door, she knocked and heard a familiar voice say, "Come in."

She opened the door and walked in. Her father was sitting behind his desk, a surprisingly old, nondescript one that he had been using for as long as Victoria could remember. She was used to his office, but those who paid her father a visit were frequently surprised by it. He was a simple man who never forgot about his and her mother's humble beginnings and the amount of work it took to get to where they were. He had no interest in the trappings of his position. Besides the desk, he had several old metal filing cabinets along the wall and two high-back chairs across from his desk. His two extravagances were a wine refrigerator, stocked with a variety of the wines they imported, and nearly a dozen large, high-quality photographs that chronicled her parents' story.

Her father waved her in and pointed to a chair while he continued his telephone conversation. As she waited for him to finish, Victoria spent her time looking at the pictures. The first one showed them in Uganda, surrounded by a large group of children. They spent much of their early years together doing mission work around the world. While on one of their earlier trips, her father met a merchant who had sold a few of the local products to him. He carried them home and shared them with family and friends. That was the beginning of Van Hough Industries. Other photos showed the happy couple in such locations as Armenia, Mongolia, and Lebanon. In each picture, her parents were holding hands and had enormous smiles on their faces. Victoria's heart sunk as she examined them more closely. Over the years, the smiles had turned to ones of contempt. She tried to think of the last time she thought her parents had been truly happy, but couldn't. It was at least ten years ago. She wasn't sure what happened, but their relationship had turned, in Victoria's opinion, into a dysfunctional one bordering on toxic.

Victoria's relationship with her father, on the other hand, couldn't have been more different. Throughout her life, he had been loving and understanding. He had nurtured her, taught her, and encouraged her. He was her biggest fan and most loving critic. The sound of him hanging up the telephone brought her back to reality as he got up, moved to the door, and closed it. He and Victoria had a routine to their interactions while in the office. When around employees or when there were open doors, he was Jim and she was Victoria, and Jim was the boss. But when either of them had personal things to discuss, they closed the door. Now, as her father closed the door, she wondered about the topic of conversation. Instead of sitting behind his desk, he took the seat next to her and turned his chair so that he was face-to-face with her.

"Oh, such a serious face," Victoria said playfully to her dad. "I thought we were talking business, but I guess I was wrong."

"We haven't gotten a chance to talk much lately, so I was wondering what's going on in your life." He had that look on his face like the cat that caught the canary, so Victoria knew he had something specific in mind. She squinted her eyes as she looked at him, hoping to gain some insight from his body language. Nothing. "Here lately, your mother has been rather gruff, and you have been walking on air. That can only tell me one thing."

Victoria instantly knew where he was going. A picture of Nate flashed before her eyes, and a huge smile came over her face. "That's my girl," her dad said proudly. "Do you know how much I love seeing you happy?" She could see it in his eyes, and it made her happy, too. She and her father used to talk about her relationships, the happy ones anyway. But they had been so infrequent lately. Of course, she never shared the details with him that she did with Sue, but her father always had great insight to offer her.

"Dad, you have no idea," she said, scooting to the edge of her chair as if telling a secret to her best friend. "Nate is a really great guy. So loving. And he's so dedicated to those children. I just love his life story." She felt like she was gushing, so she stopped herself.

"From the first time I heard him speak, I knew he was destined to do great things. He talked about his childhood and his passion for helping other children. I was drawn to him and had to help him. Now I'm so glad that you two are making a go of it."

Victoria spent the next ten minutes telling her dad about their time together so far. She was so excited she felt like a schoolgirl all over again. He laughed and beamed with pride as she shared details. After she finished, she said, "Well, you know me, Dad. I'm a realist, and I know we have an uphill climb with lots of challenges, but I see so much potential!"

He shook his head and reached out, taking her hand in his, and she knew the wisdom was coming. "Honey, you are so smart and so analytical. Those qualities serve you well in work and in your personal life. But sometimes you have to push that aside. Sometimes things don't make sense to your analytical brain. There are too many obstacles stacked up against you, and your brain holds you back from something that could be really special. Let your heart be your guide. Open up. Be a little reckless and see where it leads you. You just might find something really wonderful."

He pulled her in for a hug, and she whispered, "Thanks, Dad. I will, I promise."

CHAPTER EIGHT

She pushed the button on her visor to activate the gate, and as it slowly creaked open, it reminded Victoria of how she felt. She let out a slow, deep breath, feeling the soreness that penetrated her muscles to her bones. And the way she slept on her neck last night didn't help, either.

She pushed the accelerator hard causing the tires to squeal a little and made a right turn onto the main road, headed to Van Hough Industries. This time of year she had to push her body to the limit. With only a few exceptions, she worked from sunrise until well after sunset. Even through the last few years, while she finished her education, she spent her winter break working with her father. He taught her everything he had learned about the business. Victoria knew he had dreams of passing the company to her, but he was always careful to ensure it was her decision. He never tried to force her to work there. Victoria, if you don't want to work here, I understand. I want you to pursue a career that will make you happy no matter what that path is, he had told her frequently. She knew he'd meant it, and she loved him for it. But she loved working for the company and contributing to its success. It was her choice.

Now that she was the vice president of purchasing, she

had full responsibility for ensuring a steady stream of products into the company. It was exhausting. At the stoplight, she pulled her visor down and carefully examined herself in the mirror, looking for bags under her eyes or the hint of crow's-feet "Nope. Still fabulous," she said as the light turned green and she flipped the visor up and continued on. Her father was out of town on business but called in frequently to help keep things on track. His guidance was so important to her, both personally and professionally. She sped up the entrance ramp to the highway, wanting to get to work, and settled in before his first call. Luckily, he was two time zones behind, so she had a little time to spare.

As she sped down the highway, she stretched her neck out, tilting it back and forth, causing it to crack several times. She took her hand, raised her long blond hair, and rubbed the back of her head. It was bad enough that she felt so run-down physically, but dealing with her mother exhausted her mentally. The constant interference in her personal life was completely unacceptable. But Victoria knew that addressing this subject with her mother was impossible. Even with the support of her father, it would be a monumental task. Just the thought of it made her clench her teeth, and she became frustrated with the pace of traffic, swerving in and out, passing cars as she went.

Her mother had done some inappropriate things before, but a couple nights ago was way over the line. How could she have invited Carter to the house without consulting her first? To say it shocked her when he walked out of the shadows was a colossal understatement. He was the last person she wanted to see, especially after having such a wonderful time with Nate. Yet there he was, on his knees, professing to be a better man. But she didn't care what he had to say. She was fully prepared to break it off with him. Then why did she allow him to stay in her life? That was a question she may never be able to answer. The best she could figure was that Carter was like an old shoe. He was broken-in and comfortable. But old shoes weren't jerks. And they didn't hurt your feelings, so that was where the analogy broke down. After a few minutes of thought on the subject, she was no closer to understanding it.

***

Victoria opened the door to her office expecting to turn the light on, but as it swung forward, the artificial light from the overhead fixtures flooded the hallway.

"Good morning, sunshine!" came a voice from the high-backed armchair across from her desk. She couldn't see its occupant, but immediately knew it was her best friend Sue.

"Ugh. Don't you have some computer stuff to take care of?" she said as she rounded the corner and worked her way to her desk chair. She pulled it out, dumped her purse and computer bag on the desk with a thud, and slumped in the chair, putting her head down on the desk. It was obvious who the morning person was.

"Vic, you look like hell. Were you up all night?" she said, using a shortened version of her name. Sue was the only person who called her that.

She reached up, pushed aside her hair, and peeked up at her while still keeping her head firmly planted on her desk. "You have no idea. If I told you what happened the other night, you would never believe me."

"Try me," she said as Victoria finally sat up in her chair. Sue reached her arm out and handed her a hot cup of coffee, causing her to perk up some. "As much as I want to hear your story about last night, I have to hear about your date with Nate first! Tell me everything."

With only the mention of his name, Victoria sat up straight in the chair and smiled. It was the best she had felt all morning.

"Look at you, Vic! All I did was say his name and you look like you are on top of the world."

"Oh my gosh, Sue, I am! It was amazing." As Victoria

told her the story, she removed her coat and unpacked her laptop to prepare for her day. She started by telling her about her hospital adventure. As she progressed through the story, Sue added a healthy dose of "Are you serious?" and "That's amazing!"

"And those kids! I was in tears," she said and noticed that Sue was getting a little misty-eyed just hearing the story. "One little boy was only six. He was so cute, I wanted to eat him up."

"This guy can't be real. I have to meet him for myself to believe it," Sue said, feigning skepticism at his existence.

"Oh, he's real, and adorable. His green eyes . . . I don't know what comes over me. They are mesmerizing."

"Did you kiss him yet?"

"I wish! Maybe soon, I hope."

Sue's expression turned more serious as something crossed her mind. "I don't mean to take us down," Sue said as she stood up, walked over to the door, and looked outside for anyone who could hear this part of the conversation. Having seen that the coast was clear, she continued. "But what about your mom? Is he 'approved'?" she asked in a hushed voice as she used air quotes around the word "approved."

"Not even close," Victoria responded with a sigh. "No chance that will ever happen. He is a surgical resident and has financed nearly his entire education. There is no way she would ever accept him." These words took all the air out of the room and the two women sat in silence sipping on their coffee. Finally, the quiet was broken when Paige, Victoria's assistant, entered the room.

"Ms. Victoria. Sorry to bother you, but Mr. Van Hough is on the phone."

"Thanks, Paige. Sue, hang out for a minute," she said and picked up the phone on her desk, punching one button. "Good morning! I'm not sure 'pumpkin' is the most professional thing you can call me, but yes. I'm doing fine," she said and flashed Sue a smile. "When are you coming home? Thursday? Good. I need your help with Mother. We'll talk about it when you get home." Victoria was silent for a minute or two and finished the conversation saying, "Okay. Send me the meeting invite and passcode and I'll be there. Talk to you then." She hung up the phone and turned her attention back to Sue.

"OMG, you still have so much to tell me," Sue said, realizing they were running out of their morning gossip time. She was the head of IT and needed to get to work. "What happened the other night?"

Victoria adjusted herself in her chair long enough to see Sue getting impatient at the delay. "Come on, already!"

Victoria laughed and said, "You know I was with Nate and then went home." Sue nodded. "When I got home, my mother ambushed me again to give me a hard time about not talking to Carter."

"Vic," she said, looking around again. "You need to get her out of your personal life."

"Oh, I know. It gets worse. After she gave me a hard time about Carter, he came around the corner."

A look of disbelief came over her face as she said, "Wait, what? Carter was at your house? How?"

"My mother invited him over."

"Vic! You have to take your life back, girl!"

"Easier said than done, but I'm going to get my dad to help when he gets back on Thursday. This has to change."

Sue was still shaking her head when she got up to leave the room. When she got to the door, she turned around and said, "Are you going to continue seeing Nate?"

"Absolutely! We're going out again on Thursday night."

"Your dad comes back and you are going out with Nate again. What a great day. I expect a full report. See you at lunch."

As Sue closed her office door, neither woman knew the utter devastation that Thursday would bring.

CHAPTER NINE

"Where am I going?" she asked herself as she looked at the GPS showing just two more miles. She hadn't been to this part of the city in quite a while, and never at this time of the evening. Nate was being Nate and wouldn't tell her what they were doing, but that was one of the things she liked about him. He had an adventurous side and so did she. When they texted about their date, he only provided her with the coordinates, but as she pulled into the parking lot, she had more of an idea regarding what he had in mind. In front of her was an old brick building displaying an ancient-looking neon sign that read, *Simpson Go Kart Racing*. She had a variety of experiences throughout her lifetime, but this was not one of them. As she pulled into the parking stall, she noticed Nate standing near the front door. A light above the door shone down on him, giving him an angelic appearance. The sight made her feel warm inside. It was the feeling of pure happiness. Dates had been scarce between them. Nate was finishing up his surgical residency, and she was busy at work. So when they got together, they had to make the time count. Including today, they have been out three times, but Victoria felt much closer to him than their dates would indicate. She wasn't ready to use the "L" word yet, but she was developing powerful feelings for him.

She got out of the car, smoothed her jeans and top. She rarely wore clothes like these, but Nate strongly suggested this attire. After seeing their activity, she was glad she listened. She took her cell phone out and switched it off before replacing it in her back pocket. Nothing was going to interfere with her date. No distractions. Just her and Nate getting to know each other more. She liked where things were going and she didn't want anything to get in the way.

Victoria's excitement showed as she covered the distance between her and Nate in a near sprint, landing in his arms with a solid hug. He felt so good. His arms were so strong wrapped around her—and his smell. She couldn't get enough. When she backed away, she finally greeted him with an enthusiastic "Hi!"

"Hi, Victoria. It's really nice to see you again. Thanks for coming."

"I love spending time with you," she said as she took his hand in hers. "What's on the agenda?"

"Follow me," he said and opened the door for her, pointing in the building. "I've heard that you have a bit of a lead foot and may like speed. I figured this would be perfect for you."

"Well, I've heard you are a sore loser, so hopefully no one is crying when we're done," she said and gave him a big smile when he looked her way.

"I see you are a little competitive, too," he said, smiling back at her.

They walked to an area with a sign that said *Safety Briefing*, and after several other people joined their group, a young man stepped to the front.

"Hi, everyone. My name is Todd, and I'll be giving you a safety briefing. Please pay attention. These may be go-karts, but they are powerful and we don't want anyone getting hurt today."

Victoria settled directly in front of Nate and she noticed that he leaned into her back, looking over her right shoulder.

She could feel his breath on her neck. He wrapped his arms around her waist, pulling her closer as the briefing proceeded. This was a bold gesture, but openly welcomed. She told him so by pushing back against his chest, snuggling into his arms and holding his arms with hers. She never wanted him to let her go.

Todd went on. "Don't get out of the go-kart . . ." *blah blah*. "Raise your hand . . ." *blah blah*. When Todd asked if there were questions, it surprised her since she couldn't remember any of the instructions he had given. Oh well. She'll figure it out.

"Okay. Let's get your helmets and put you into your go-karts." He led the way out the back door and into an area where about a dozen go-karts were waiting. All with running engines. It sounded like a bunch of yard equipment and reminded her of grass-cutting day on the estate. Todd passed around the helmets, and Nate held out his hands for Victoria's helmet. Victoria removed a hair tie from the back pocket of her jeans and put her hair into a low ponytail. After putting her helmet on for her, Nate noticed a few wild strands of hair were still flowing across her face and he swept them aside, tucking them in gently. *He's so damn sweet*, she thought.

"So what do I get when I win?" he said with cool confidence.

"When you win? You can't be serious. When I win, I have a laundry list of things I want."

"Well, when I win, all I want is a kiss."

"Interesting. That happens to be one thing on my list."

"If that's what you want, we can just skip the dramatics and go right to it," he said, pulling her close and moving in for a kiss. Just before their lips met, she slid her hand between them with her palm resting on his lips.

"Not so fast. I changed my mind. You are going to have to earn it on the track."

"As you wish, m'lady," he said and made a large sweeping motion with his arm, landing across his waist as he bowed to her. She curtsied back, and the game was on.

Nate quickly put his helmet on as they moved to their respective go-karts. Once seated, she noticed that everyone else was fastening their seat belts, so she did the same. Looking down, she could see only one pedal. She assumed it was the accelerator. No worries, she wouldn't need a brake since she planned to go full throttle the entire way around the track. She saw that luck was with her as she was seated in a car in the second row and Nate was in the third. She turned, looked at him, and blew him a kiss, just as they gave the command to start. She pushed down, forcing the pedal to the floorboard and the go-kart lurched forward, striking the car in front of her.

"Sorry!" she yelled to the teen behind the wheel who turned around and gave her a dirty look, saying, "It's not bumper cars, moron!" *Ouch*, she thought as the teen pulled away. When she looked to her left, much to her disappointment, she saw that Nate had somehow pulled even with her and she smashed the pedal down at the same time as him. Both karts leapt forward with Victoria taking a slight lead. Off into the first turn they went, bumping and grinding. The karts were surprisingly fast, but Victoria was not letting up for even a second. Down the straight they went, with Victoria managing to get in front of Nate. She stayed there for the better part of two laps, taunting him by slowing down, then speeding up and pulling away. She obviously had a faster go-kart and enjoyed teasing him.

By the third lap, she had built a sizable lead on him and planned to coast to victory. Unfortunately, karma had other plans. As they entered the last turn, with the finish line in sight, Victoria felt a tremendous bang from behind that caught her by surprise. The force of the impact caused her go-kart to veer hard to the right and crash into the tire barrier that lined the track. She looked to her left in time to see her teen friend drive by, holding up his arm with his middle finger extended. "I guess he decided they are bumper cars after all," she said to herself. "Little jerk."

To her disappointment, out of the corner of her eye, she saw Nate go flying by on his way to the finish line. "Damn it!" she yelled. Just before crossing the finish line, she saw him slow down, then creep across to end the race. Victoria straightened out her kart and eased it over the finish line in last place. It wasn't the ending she had hoped for, but since he won, she was getting a kiss, which was all she wanted, anyway. "Everyone is a winner," she said to herself as she came to a stop in the kart corral. She unbuckled herself and stood up just as Nate reached her. He faced her and wrapped his arms around her.

"To the victor go the spoils," she said as she cocked her head and waited for him to move in for the kiss she had been wanting. They got closer, and she closed her eyes. Just before their lips met, the visors on their helmets met, stopping their forward progress cold. The sound of plastic on plastic caused her to open her eyes and see what happened. He, too, saw their dilemma, and they both laughed. "Just my luck," she said, then removed her helmet, handing it to Nate. They went in and handed back their helmets, then moved to the middle of the room. Victoria took her ponytail down and ran her fingers through her hair to smooth it out.

Out of nowhere, Nate came around her front, ran his hand along her face and around to her neck, putting his other hand around her waist and pulling her close to him. She only had a second to recognize what was going on, and she closed her eyes in anticipation. Their lips met, and she felt how warm and wet they were as he pulled her even closer. Although she wished it would have gone on longer, after a moment, he pulled away a few inches and looked into her eyes.

"That was better than I ever imagined it would be," he said as he stroked her cheek. Victoria was frozen in the moment. He leaned forward and gave her another brief kiss before pulling away and taking her hand. She was walking on air.

"We should probably get something to eat," he said, breaking the trance he had her under.

"Sure," she said, barely able to get her words out.

"How about hot dogs?" he said, pointing to the menu board above the small grill built into the go-kart building.

Victoria didn't follow any special diet, and she had tried her share of dishes that were bad for you, but she had no intentions of eating a hot dog, which she noted was neither hot nor a dog. "How about a salad?" she replied.

"Absolutely," he said as they split up. He moved to the counter to order the food, while she walked to the picnic tables, which occupied the center of the building, and took a seat. She busied herself while waiting for Nate to return by doing one of her favorite pastimes: people watching. To her right, she saw a fresh crop of drivers getting their orientation from Todd. They were obviously much better at listening to his instructions than she was. There were teens everywhere, including the one who took her out at the end of their race. Lucky for him he was hanging with his friends or she may have gone over there and chatted with him about manners or good driving habits. "Oh, who am I kidding? I should thank him. After all, I got the kiss I wanted," she said out loud and the thought of Nate's soft lips made her smile. She looked to the left and could see cars coming and going in the parking lot, their headlights shining through the windows into the building. Just as Nate sat down carrying a tray of food, Victoria glanced out the window again, squinting to get a better look.

"Strange," she said.

"What's so strange?" Nate asked as he began placing the food on the table along with the drinks.

"I could have sworn I saw Sue's car pull into the parking lot."

"Who is Sue and why would she be here?" he asked as he took a French fry and sat across from her. The bench groaned under him as he settled in.

"She's my best friend," she said with her eyes still locked

on the action. She strained to see through the windows that looked out into the parking lot.

"How would she know you are here and why would she come?" he said before smiling and continuing, "It's probably because you made me sound so irresistible that she had to come see for herself," he said and chuckled.

She turned her head, looking at Nate, and smiled. "If you must know, I told her you were adorable. But there is still an outside chance you may be an ax murderer, so I gave her the GPS coordinates you gave me."

Nate held his arms out and rolled his eyes back in his head. "I said killed by an ax murderer, not a zombie," she replied and rolled her eyes, too. "Besides, you can't be too careful these days. I always tell her exactly where I'm going and who I will be with, just in case."

Nate stuffed several French fries into his mouth as Victoria turned her attention back to the windows. "It was her!" she exclaimed just as Nate turned to see a woman in her twenties enter the building and look around. "Sue! Over here!" she yelled, causing Sue to turn toward the voice she obviously recognized. Their eyes met and Sue quickly made her way over to the table. Victoria knew Sue well and could see she was very upset. Her eyes were swollen and red as if she had been crying. "What's wrong?" she asked as Sue arrived at their table. "If you wanted to meet Nate, you could have just asked," she said, trying to lighten the dark mood she sensed in her friend. Sue extended her arms and grabbed Victoria, hugging her and holding her tight. She stepped back, looking at Nate.

"Nice to meet you, Nate," she whispered, extending her hand to shake his. "Vicky, I need to talk to you now, please. Let's go," she insisted and grabbed her hand, pulling her across the room toward the door.

Victoria turned to look at Nate as she was being dragged to the door. "Start eating, I'll be back in a few minutes."

She barely completed the sentence as the exterior door closed behind her. "Sue, please tell me what's going on. You are scaring me now." But Sue didn't respond. As they got to her car, she unlocked the doors, and the two got in, closing the doors behind them. Sue turned to Victoria, who took the passenger seat and reached out to take both her hands. Sue's lips quivered, and she struggled to speak. "Please. What's going on?"

Sue looked into Victoria's eyes, and a sudden tsunami of tears came flooding out. She openly sobbed as Victoria tried to console her friend about some yet unknown catastrophe. "Vic, I have to tell you something," she said in an unsuccessful attempt to compose herself. As the next wave of tears hit, Sue said, "Your dad—"

"What about my dad?" Victoria asked, cutting her off. Panic was building in her voice. "He's flying home from Denver." She looked at her watch, noting the time. "In fact, he should have landed already. Is everything okay?" She felt her throat go dry before she could finish.

Sue wiped away her tears with her sweater before continuing, "They lost radar contact with his plane shortly after takeoff."

"What?" She looked around the car to buy time to collect her thoughts. "He is an excellent pilot. Maybe he had mechanical problems and landed somewhere for repairs," she said, pleading for her suggestion to be correct. All Sue could muster was to shake her head back and forth. "No, Sue! Don't do that. You don't know!" She took her hands and gently put them on the sides of Sue's face to stop her from saying no. Tears spilled out of Victoria's eyes. "Sue . . . don't do this to me, please," she whispered as Sue quietly sobbed.

Sue turned her head to stare out the windshield. "The state police found the wreckage Vic, I'm so sorry."

"No! You know my dad, Sue! He's a survivor! He's okay . . ." she said with her voice trailing off. "Look at me." Sue turned and looked and saw the utter despair in her friend's eyes. "He's fine. You'll see," she said, sitting up straight in the seat and wiping the tears away.

"Vic. They confirmed there were no survivors," she said, reaching for her hands again. Victoria was numb inside and shook uncontrollably.

Victoria whispered, "How can this be? Is this true? Sue, please . . ." and when she saw her friend nodding up and down, the gravity of the situation hit her. Her heart was beating out of her chest and she had trouble catching her breath. "What am I going to do now?"

"I'll help you. Whatever you need, I'll be there for you," she said and squeezed her friend's hands tight. "Let me drive you home. You shouldn't be behind the wheel."

Victoria reached into her pocket and took her cell phone out, switching it on. It came to life and notified her that she had missed five phone calls: two from Sue and three from her mother. "Does she know?" Sue nodded yes.

"She wanted me to tell you. She thought it would be better."

Victoria started to cry. She reached for the handle and opened the car door.

"Vic, where are you going? You can't drive. Let me drive you home."

"I have to go. Thank you for being so compassionate, Sue. You are an amazing friend. I love you."

"I love you, too. Please be careful and text me later."

She closed the car door and looked around the parking lot. After spotting her own car, she walked to it. Her mind was swimming. Was she dreaming? Did this really happen? How was this possible? She opened the car door and sat in the driver's seat, pulling down the visor and looking at herself. In disgust, she slammed the visor up and rested her head on the steering wheel, crying. "Dad . . . what am I going to do without you?" She started her car and backed out. She drove through the parking lot to the exit and before leaving, took out her phone to send a text.

I'm coming over. I need to talk. Within a minute she received a response. *Fine. See you soon.*

She pulled out, making a right, and headed to the

highway.

***

She turned right, entering the driveway, and pulled up to the security gate. After waiting a minute, the gate swung open, and she drove up to the house, parking in the circle drive in front. *This was way overdue*, she thought as she pulled her visor down, fluffed her long hair, trying to make herself look presentable. After a long sigh, she exited her car and headed to the front door of the house. As she stepped onto the front porch, a light came on and the front door opened.

"To what do I owe the pleasure of your visit?" Carter asked. "I haven't heard from you in a while." He looked at Victoria as she became visible in the porch light. "Wow, Vicky, you look like crap!"

"I have had the worst night of my life."

Carter reached out to take her hand, but she pulled away. "No, Carter."

"I don't understand," he said with hesitation in his voice. "Do you want to come in?"

"No, I don't." She took a deep breath and reached down deep in her soul. This conversation was a long time coming. "Carter, we're over. I don't want to see you anymore."

There was a period of stunned silence as her words sunk in. "But, Vicky, I—"

"There!" she said before he could even finish. "You don't care what I think, feel, or say. And stop calling me that!" she said with surprising force.

"But we are so right for each other." He reached for her hand again. She swatted it away.

"I can't believe you would even say that. We are so wrong for each other. We have nothing in common and don't share the same goals. You don't respect me or my opinion. And honestly, the only reason we were together up to this point is my mother!" Putting her feelings into words gave her satisfaction.

"You are making a big mistake."

"No, Carter, staying with you would have been the biggest mistake of my life. Goodbye." She turned and walked across the porch, down the stairs, and back to her car. She never looked back as she got in, started the engine, and drove down the driveway. When she got to the end, she stopped, waiting for the emotions to overwhelm her. To her surprise, they didn't. She never felt more confident in a decision. But before she could continue, the gravity of the loss of her father swamped her, and she looked through teary eyes as she made a right turn and headed home.

***

During the drive home, Victoria tried to hold it together with various levels of success. She rounded the corner and headed up the driveway, and as the gate to their family compound opened, she thought about her mother and how this was impacting her. She imagined her sitting at the dining room table, smoking, drinking tea, and being consoled by Helen. She expected the number of tears she shed would have been similar to her own. Although their marriage had been strained for the last several years, she knew they had spent the better part of two decades hopelessly in love. She thought back to the pictures on her father's office walls. Surely the love they showed was real. Her parents had worked endlessly to build a life together, through many challenges, but had enjoyed many good times as well. Even with all the animosity between them over the last several years, she was sure her mother would be taking this badly. As she switched her car off, the sight of her father's empty parking spot made her cry again and she sat in the car, letting the tears flow.

After a few minutes, she composed herself. She wiped away the tears and got out of the car, plodding to the door leading into the house. Through the doorway, down the hall and up the stairs she went, stopping at the top to listen. It would not have surprised her to hear crying in the distance. Sounds carried well through these hallways, enhanced by the walnut wainscoting and hardwood floors. She heard nothing. As she took the hallway to the right that lead to the dining room, she heard soft voices that built as she got closer. Her mother's voice was unmistakable and when she heard her break out into a cackle-like laugh, she stopped in her tracks. What could possibly be so funny coming on the eve of her father's death? By referring to the event as her father's death, was she accepting the finality of it? The thought made her want to cry again, but she fought back the tears and quietly sniffled.

"Victoria, dear? Is that you? Please come and join us," her mother's voice came from the dining room. It was surprisingly strong. Victoria couldn't detect any cracking. As she entered the room, the scene was as she imagined it just a few minutes prior. Her mother was sitting at the long, custom oak table, lighting another cigarette. Her cup of tea was on the table and Helen was sitting two chairs to her left. Absent though were the puffy eyes or pile of tissues near them, which would normally indicate tears and sadness. Helen stood up and pulled out the chair between them, beckoning her to come and sit. Instead, she selected a seat on the other side of the table. Helen pushed in both her and the other chair.

"I'll leave you two alone, ma'am," she said as she headed toward the door. "My condolences about your father, Ms. Victoria." She lowered her head and left the room.

"I assume Sue got to you tonight?" Victoria nodded her head. "I thought it would be better that you hear it from her and not me. I understand that our relationship can be strained sometimes, so I hope you are okay with my decision." She continued to puff on her cigarette and Victoria noted how steady her hands were. Not what she expected from someone who had just lost her husband.

"What's going on with you, Mother?" Victoria asked with a touch of annoyance in her voice.

"What do you mean, dear?"

"I've been falling apart all night. I can't stop crying, my head is pounding and my stomach is in knots. You are in here drinking tea, laughing and acting like nothing happened."

"Now, Victoria, everyone grieves in their own way and in their own time. Helen and I were just sharing a humorous story about your father."

"You will have to excuse me if I don't believe you," she said, raising her voice slightly.

"I understand that you are upset, but you will not take that tone of voice with me. I am still your mother."

Normally Victoria backed down, choosing to accept that as her mother the title brought a high level of respect. But tonight, she was itching for a fight and all respect was gone.

"You're not sad at all that he's gone. You have been waiting for this. Looking forward to the day when you would control everything! Save your faking for the funeral."

The verbal attack must have struck a nerve with her mother and she sprung to her feet slamming her fist down on the table causing her teacup to spill. The chair she was sitting in fell backwards with a thud onto the hardwood floor.

"You want to know the truth? Your father was a philanderer who cared more about fulfilling his personal needs outside the marriage! So if you think I will shed even a single tear for him, you better think again!" There was rage in her voice.

"Don't you dare disparage his name on the back of your marital problems! He was a good man. He cared about others, which is more than I can say about you."

"That was the problem, Victoria. He cared about everyone else except me." Suddenly the rage was gone, and a smile came over her face. "Denver," she said with a long pause. "How apropos. Did you ever ask yourself why he spent so much time in Denver? It wasn't because he was importing tea."

73

"You lie! Take that back now!"

Her mother laughed softly, then turned around and righted the fallen chair before sitting back down and looking her in the eyes with a laser focus that made Victoria very uncomfortable. "I strongly suggest you go up to your room before either of us says something that we can't take back. You have no idea what kind of fire you are playing with." Victoria heard, in her mother's voice, a level of hatred she had never heard before. It scared her. She turned to leave just as Helen entered the room with a rag to clean up the spilled tea. She made her way to her suite, feeling that anger had now replaced her sorrow.

CHAPTER TEN

Things were not any better now than the night of her father's death. After their altercation, Victoria had not spoken to her mother, and she wasn't sure when she would again. The way she disparaged her father was almost unforgivable. And the hateful way in which she spoke was disturbing. Victoria could feel the rage in her mother that night. It was something she had never experienced with her before. Since then, her mother had directed Helen to completely clean out all of her father's clothes from the home, and she had his car towed from the airport in Denver to a used car lot and listed for sale. But the biggest dagger, in Victoria's mind, was when she cleaned out his office at work and moved herself in, declaring that effective immediately, she was the new CEO of Van Hough Industries. "We have to keep the company running, dear," was her response when Victoria questioned her. She had a troubling feeling there was more to come.

She took a seat on the bench outside the front door of the estate, waiting for her ride. Her father's wake was today and her mother arranged for a limo to take them, but she was the last person Victoria wanted to be with right now. So she asked Sue to go with her. She looked down the driveway and recognized Sue's car as it pulled up to the gate. She took out her cell phone to activate the gate, but it opened on its own before she could call up the app. She shook her head, then walked down to the circle drive and waited for her to arrive.

When the car came to a stop, she heard the door lock click, and she opened the passenger door and got in.

"Hi, Vic," Sue said sympathetically.

They embraced warmly, before Victoria put her seat belt on and Sue started the drive back toward the road. As they passed the gate, she said, "Remind me to get that gate fixed. It opened before I got the app up and let you in."

"I'll cut you some slack today since you have a lot on your mind, but I'm the one who designed the security system for the estate, remember? I have administrator access to everything," she said as she pulled onto the main road.

"I forgot. Sorry. I have a lot on my mind. Thanks for picking me up. If I had to be in that limo with my mother . . ."

"It would have been ugly," Sue completed her sentence. "Did she leave already?"

"Oh yeah. Hours ago. She wanted to get there really early to make everything look perfect. It makes me sick the way she tries to make it look like they were the loving couple, with her the grieving wife. Sue, I never realized how deep my mother's hatred ran. My father hid it so well that I never suspected."

"It must be hard for you. How are you doing?"

"I'm so lost: personally, professionally. It's horrible. He was my father, boss, mentor, and my best friend. I don't know what I'm going to do."

The darkness of her words hung over them as Sue continued the drive to the funeral home where her father's wake was taking place.

"How is Nate? Is he coming today?"

"Honestly, I don't know. He's been really sweet through

this whole thing, and sent me flowers with a nice note. I know he's hurt by this, too, since my dad was so important in mentoring him. I just think he doesn't want to intrude, since our relationship is so new."

"But you guys hit it off so well. And he adores you. You really need to talk to him," she said.

"How do you know he adores me?"

"He told me! When I went back into the go-kart place to tell him what happened, he was gushing over you. He felt so bad, but said he understood why you had to leave. I told him you went home, but if he knew where you really went, it would upset him, I'm sure."

"I know, but, Sue, it had to be done. I couldn't go on living a lie anymore. I'm just sorry I didn't do it sooner."

"I'm so proud of you," Sue said, before pivoting back to the more important topic of conversation. "You really need to get with Nate again. Don't leave him hanging, Vic. Guys like that don't wait around very long," she advised. "Oh, darn. Look at this traffic." Victoria looked up to see a long line of traffic that had formed in the right lane. About six blocks up, a police officer was standing in the street directing traffic.

"Oh my gosh, Vic, this is traffic for your dad's service. I'll try to get you close to the front door and then go park."

"Thanks."

Sue trudged along through lines of traffic until making a right turn into the parking lot of the funeral home. She stopped at the front door and Victoria got out. The car pulled away as she walked up the steps and entered the building. She was astonished by the number of people there. They gathered in small groups, filling the room and spilling out the front door. Between the groups, she saw a sign that directed attendees to the left, and a line had formed leading into the main viewing room. She weaved her way through the crowds and to the main room. She recognized many of the people there but didn't have the energy to talk to them yet.

At the front of the room, she saw a life-sized picture of her father's torso on an easel. Seeing it caused a large catch to form in her throat and she wondered how she would get through this evening. Numerous flower arrangements filled the front and surrounded her father's picture. Chairs were set up in the center, each containing an important member of the community, there to pay their last respects. As the sea of people flowed back and forth, she saw her mother. She was standing next to the picture, decked out in a black dress with a veil and a silk scarf in her hand. As she talked to several people, she used the scarf to blot her eyes. Occasionally, she sniffled and her body heaved up and down while people patted her on the shoulder or gave her a hug. The sight made her furious, but she was determined to keep this event cordial. She took a deep breath and made her way to her mother's side. Her mother saw her coming and held her arms out, beckoning her forward.

"Oh, Victoria, dear. I'm so glad you're here. Isn't this an amazing turnout? Your father was beloved by so many." She pulled Victoria into position next to her.

A barrel-chested man was next in line and greeted her mother with a warm hug. "I'm so sorry for your loss, Alice. Jim was a good man. I will dearly miss him."

"Thanks for saying that, Sam. Yes, he will," she said, then blotted her eyes and sniffled. "Oh, I'd like to introduce you to our daughter, Victoria." She held her hand out, and he shook it.

"I'm sorry, Ms. Victoria," he said and then shuffled along to allow the line to creep forward.

Over the next two hours, the line moved along, inch by inch. Some people she knew or recognized, but many she didn't. They were a who's who of the most important people in the city: mayors, police chiefs, county commissioners, business leaders, and many more. She was never so proud to be his daughter and never so embarrassed to be standing next to her mother. Nevertheless, for the sake of peace, she kept up the charade, watching her mother pretend to be sad and wipe away imaginary tears. The tears Victoria shed, on the other hand, were real, but she did the best she could to hold them in. Those that escaped were quickly wiped away before they could disturb her makeup.

It was emotionally draining, and just when she didn't think she could take any more, she looked up and saw the next person in line was Carter. Her heart sank. She never expected him to be here.

"Oh, look who's here!" her mother exclaimed. "Carter. How nice to see you. Thanks for coming by." She looked at Victoria with a devious smile.

"I'm sorry for your loss, Mrs. Van Hough. And you, too, Victoria," he said as he turned to look at her. "Vicky, I'm so sorry I wasn't a good boyfriend for you. I was insensitive and I promise I'll change. Please forgive me."

Before Victoria could say anything, Alice made room between them and installed Carter in the space. For the next twenty minutes, she introduced Carter as her boyfriend. Every time Victoria tried to correct her, she waved her comments away with her hand, saying, "Not now dear." Twice, Carter attempted to hold her hand, but she pulled away at his touch.

As the evening wound down, the crowd thinned and Victoria could see the next few people in line. She saw Sue was up next, but she had her back to her, blocking the person behind her. She was excited to see Sue and glad she stuck around. Now she wouldn't have to ride home with her mother.

"Hi, Mrs. Van Hough. I'm sorry for your and Victoria's loss," Sue said, and as she stepped aside, Victoria could see the person standing several feet behind her, and panic set in. Their eyes met and Sue winked at her.

"Carter, would you be a dear and get Victoria a glass of water? She looks so thirsty." She pointed down a hallway to the left and continued, "The kitchen is down there. Thanks so much." And as Carter obediently stepped out of line, Victoria grabbed her hand and squeezed it tight, mouthing *thank you.*

Sue continued to hang out just off of Victoria's shoulder as the line moved. Victoria held her breath as a deep voice said, "I'm sorry for your loss, Mrs. Van Hough. Your husband was a great man. He was my mentor, and I wouldn't be where I am today without his help."

Mrs. Van Hough looked up and, not recognizing him, gave him her standard "Thank you. He will be sorely missed," before shuffling him down the line past Victoria, preventing her from saying anything to him.

As he passed her, Sue slid into the space previously occupied by Carter, blocking her view to the left. She pushed Victoria hard in the back as she said, "Look over there, Mrs. Van Hough, isn't that Mayor Johnston?" Victoria could hear her reply as she walked away, following Nate down the hallway to the back of the building. As he stepped outside into the parking lot, Victoria followed, grabbing his hand and startling him.

"Nate, please wait. Can we talk?"

"Sure."

"I'm sorry I haven't called you. This has been so hard on me, and with the responsibilities I have at our business, I've been swamped."

"Victoria, you don't owe me any explanation. I understand. Whenever I spoke to your father about you, he always gushed. I know you two were very close and it must be a devastating loss for you."

Hearing the deep sincerity in his voice caused all the emotions she kept bottled up today to come rushing out, and she began to quietly cry. Nate took his handkerchief from his pocket and gently wiped away her tears before opening his arms and offering her a warm, sympathetic hug. She moved into his arms and felt them close around her. He made her feel so comforted. All her problems seemed for the moment to fade away.

She was too comfortable to notice the sound of the back door close as someone else exited the building.

"Vicky? What's going on here?"

She broke their embrace and whirled around to see Carter, who was now standing in front of her. "Can I ask what you are doing out here with him?"

"Him has a name, and it's Nate Robinson. Who the heck are you?" he asked.

"I'm her fiancé. We've been together for six months, but I'm not sure what business that is of yours, Mr. Robinson."

Victoria, caught by surprise, tried to intervene. "Carter, wait. Stop." But they pushed her aside as the men sized each other up.

"Fiancé? And you have been dating for six months?"

"No, Nate," Victoria said, but couldn't get between the two men.

"Yes, so thanks for coming and paying your respects, but it's probably time for you to move on."

It took a minute for the information to register in Nate's mind, but then he turned around and walked away, just as Carter took Victoria's hand and led her back into the funeral home. As the door slammed behind them, Victoria cried again. Not for the loss of her father, although the sadness of that still weighed heavily on her heart, but she cried because the door just cut off her best chance at a lasting love.

CHAPTER ELEVEN

The office always became silent this time of the evening. One by one, the employees of Van Hough Industries wrapped up their work for the day and transitioned their lives from work to family. Victoria imagined them picking up children from school or daycare or cooking a wonderful supper. Sometimes she was envious of those who had a normal family life. One that involved gathering around the table and eating together, going to school events, or taking family vacations. She had none of those things. For as long as she could remember, her parents' lives were all about building a business. Victoria came along early in that process and although they wanted to have more children, life just got in the way. So most of her childhood involved being with her parents while they did work things. Now she found herself repeating that same pattern. Life was work and work was life. But she didn't know what else to do. It had been a month since her father died, and she was just as lost as ever. The door to her office swung open and Sue came in, plopping down in the seat across from Victoria.

"How goes it, Vic?" Sue asked as she let out a long sigh. Her workday was over, and she was heading home. "How much longer are you staying?"

"I don't know. There is so much to do still. I can't seem to get on top of it all," she said while continuing to look down at the papers on her desk.

"Something has to change. You can't keep doing this. You have stayed late every night and are here seven days a week. It's not healthy."

"I can't let my father down. This is his business and I have to keep it going."

"Do you really think he would be happy with how you are living your life now? Vic, you don't have a life. What happened to trying to get a better work-life balance?"

"I don't know . . ." she trailed off and laid her forehead on her desk.

"You still haven't spoken to Nate, have you?" she asked, already knowing the answer.

"No," Victoria replied and gently knocked her forehead against the desk.

"What are you waiting for? He's perfect for you. You guys have a wonderful time together. You're crazy about him and he adores you."

"I know, but I haven't spoken to him directly in almost a month." She paused for a minute, lost in her thoughts. "I miss him so much," she said and raised her head back up. "Is that normal? After only a few dates, should I be feeling so empty without him? I want him to hold me and laugh with me. And those arms!" She stopped. "But the way we ended the last time I saw him. That was bad. And I've just been so busy with everything going on."

"I'm sorry, Vic. I saw him heading that way, and I couldn't get there fast enough. By the time I got to the door, you guys were coming back in the funeral home."

"It's not your fault. It's mine for not standing up and correcting the misunderstanding right there. I was just overwhelmed by the whole situation." She thought for a minute before continuing, "We've texted a few times, but I don't feel like we've gotten back on track."

"Girl, you have to fix this!"

A loud ringing came out of Sue's purse and she reached in, grabbing her cell phone. "Damn. I have to go," she said, getting up and heading to the door. "Promise me! You are going to talk to him, right?" she asked as she went through the doorway and into the hall, the ringing following her out of the office.

"I promise!" she yelled back.

Suddenly, the room was silent again, and Victoria was left to her own thoughts. She wondered, where is that woman she swore she would become after the plane crash that almost ended her life? She told herself she would insist on a better balance in her life. And she wanted a genuine relationship with someone who understood her. It was so easy the first time she texted Nate. What did she have to lose then? But life has gotten so complicated now. She fished her phone out of her purse and rolled it around in her hand. As she did, it came to life and vibrated vigorously, causing her to drop it on her desk. "Damn." She picked it up, seeing there was a new text. It made her uneasy. All this talk of texts with Nate. Could it be a sign? Is it from him? She turned it over and unlocked it. The text read: *Don't forget. YOU PROMISED! Love you!* What would she ever do without Sue?

She looked at the clock on her phone, saw it was seven o'clock, and vowed to only work one more hour before going home. She scrolled to the contact marked *Blind Date Nate* and opened it.

"It's time to make this right," she said to herself, and composed a brief text. *Nate. Can we meet and talk?* She pressed Send and put her phone on the desk, trying to refocus on her work. As she began typing, the vibration of her phone startled her, and she reached to grab her runaway phone. "Sue, if that's you again, we're going to have words," she said as she picked up her phone to look. This time, it wasn't Sue.

CHAPTER TWELVE

It felt nice to turn the tables on him and Victoria was beaming as she sat on the park bench waiting for Nate to arrive. This time, she chose the location and kept it simple. It was a beautiful day, so she decided they should meet at a park in the middle of the city. The bright sunshine and chirping songbirds added to her upbeat spirit. Unfortunately, she had to wait several days until their schedules could sync up, but that only added to her excitement. After talking with Sue, she realized Nate was perfect for her and she was letting her future pass her by. She thought back to the night on the plane when her father gave her Nate's phone number. Now look where they were. They were on the cusp of something really amazing. What made it even better for her was that it was all with her father's blessing. She had no doubt that her father would be proud of her, and the business would survive if she wasn't there seven days a week. It was time for Victoria to take back her life, and it was going to start today.

She scanned the park to bide her time until Nate arrived. It was a busy time of day with many people taking advantage of the late-season sunshine. Children laughed and screamed while enjoying the playground with their parents hovering nearby. The sight made her smile, although she would never be one of those parents. "Back up and let your children learn and explore on their own," she said, even though the playground was much too far away for her advice to be heard. Although she wasn't ready for children of her own yet, she wasn't far off and she had a good feeling about Nate in that regard. She watched him in action at the hospital and knew he would make an excellent father. *Our children would be absolutely beautiful,* she mused. The thought of her mother and the problems she may create crept into her mind, but she swept them away, thinking she will deal with that later. Besides, if she wanted to see her grandchildren, she would have to get with the program.

As wonderful thoughts filled her heart, a pair of hands wrapped around her head, covering her eyes in an adolescent game of "Guess Who." The breeze carried his scent to her nose, leaving no doubt who was behind her, and she took a deep breath. She reached up, grabbed his hands in hers, and pulled him to her, wrapping his arms around her shoulders. He reached his head forward and planted a gentle kiss on her neck, causing chills to race down her spine. She couldn't imagine anything better than this. He withdrew his arms and as she looked left, she saw him spring over the bench, landing in front before taking a seat next to her. "Wow!" she said, impressed by his grace and athletic ability. He was dressed in slacks and an amazingly soft sweater that she imagined getting lost in as he wrapped his muscular arms around her. He put his left arm around her back while taking her face in his right hand, pulling her close. She melted as his lips touched hers and they shared a warm kiss.

"I've been waiting to do that for a while," he said as he pulled his face away and settled himself on the bench. He continued to rub her shoulder gently, and she sat there, enjoying his touch.

Victoria took a deep breath before addressing the elephant in the room. "I'm so sorry for everything I've done to you. I don't know what came over me."

He turned, looking Victoria in the eyes. "Victoria, you just lost your father. He was your world. I can't imagine what that was like for you. There's no reason to apologize."

Her eyes misted up with the mention of her father. She cursed herself. This was not the time for an emotional outburst. But he was so warm and understanding. Trying to prevent him from seeing her emotions, she turned her head and stood up, saying, "Let's take a walk."

She took his hand, but as he stood up next to her, he forced her to face him. He must have sensed her feelings. "Don't be afraid to show your emotions to me. You are human." And he wrapped his arms around her, pulling her in tight. She felt so safe, and a tear escaped her eye, running down her cheek and onto his sweater. He never noticed, but she was sure it would not have mattered to him.

"So where do you want to walk?" he said, releasing his bear hug on her. They held hands and headed across the grass in the direction of the playground. As they got closer, the sound of children grew louder and louder. She led them to the swings and Victoria selected one in the middle before sitting down.

With a childlike excitement in her voice, she said, "Push me!"

Nate took up a position behind her and began pushing her on the swing. The wind blew in her face and the rhythmic sound of the creaking swing set was soothing. As he pushed her, she leaned back, looking at Nate behind her as her long hair ran across the ground under her. Upside-down Nate waved to her playfully. She closed her eyes, imagining Nate pushing their child on a swing, encouraging her to hold on tight as the imaginary child laughed uncontrollably.

Directed by Victoria, Nate took up a swing next to her and they began swinging in tandem. Slowly at first, then higher they went, each pumping harder to outdo the other. As one peaked from their forward momentum, the other worked to get higher. They called out to each other, trying to prove they were the winner. Victoria was looking at Nate when, at the peak of his forward swing, he released the chains and pushed himself out of the seat, appearing to intentionally fly off the swing. She held her breath as he successfully landed about five feet in front of the swing set. He turned toward Victoria, taking a congratulatory bow before running around the playground getting air high fives from all the unsuspecting children. He ran over to Victoria as her swing came to a stop.

"I win!" he said, holding up his arms in victory.

"You definitely did. That was impressive."

She got off the swing and reached out her hand, taking his and leading him around a tall structure connected to the swing set by a suspension bridge. They went to the metal ladder, and she began climbing up.

"Hey. Where are you going? You don't really think I can fit up there, do you?"

She turned around and gave him her best *come hither* look, knowing he could not resist. Then she turned and continued the climb to the top. Once there, she easily squeezed her slight frame through the opening before standing up and turning around to watch Nate. Fitting through was not as easy for him. He turned his body sideways and carefully slithered through the opening, making several grunting noises that caused her to laugh. Once through, he stood up and walked over to Victoria.

"I knew you could do it!" she said as she wrapped her arms around his neck and gave him a kiss as his reward. "Come over here," she said, making her way to a large ship's wheel. "Argh! Avast ye, matey," she said in her best pirate voice. "Or I'll make ye walk the plank, ye scallywag!"

"Well shiver me timbers, captain. I'm just a lily-livered landlubber. Please don't send me down to Davy Jones's locker," he said as Victoria pretended to draw her sword from an imaginary scabbard attached to her side. In a flash, Nate swept in, grabbing her hand and pulling her tight to neutralize her attack. "Now what are ye gonna do, ye salty dog? Looks like you have a mutiny on yer hands. I'll have to take ye to the poop deck for safekeeping."

Victoria burst out in laughter. "Poop deck? Is there even such a thing?"

"I have no idea. I just made it up." They both laughed. She loved he was as silly as her.

She walked over to the far side of the structure. There was a large metal slide that would take them to the ground. She sat on the top and patted the spot next to her. Nate sat down behind her and put his legs next to hers as they scooted their bottoms to the edge of the slide. When they got to the edge, gravity took control, and they headed down the slide together. He held her tight, and she raised her arms, pretending to scream like a small child. At the bottom, he helped her up, and they made their way to a nearby bench.

Once settled in, she looked at him, and a more serious tone came into her voice. "We need to talk. I want to make sure we are both on the same page, okay?"

"Sure. I think that's a great idea. What did you have in mind?"

"I want to talk about us and the possibilities, and where we're going." She took his hands in hers. "I'm really excited about a future together. I enjoy being with you. We get along great and share the same values. I really want to see where this leads us," she said, making her case, feeling like the two of them being together was the easiest decision ever.

"I have to say that I'm relieved to hear that. I thought the distance was going to be too much for you. That makes me happy."

His comments stopped her cold, and she recoiled slightly. She scrunched up her face and asked, "What are you talking about? What distance?"

"They accepted me into the pediatric surgical residency that we talked about. I leave in a week."

"No. You never told me about that," she said, shaking her head back and forth with force. There was heartbreak in her voice.

"Victoria. We talked about this. You knew I was waiting for notification of my acceptance into one of those programs. Don't you remember?"

The walls were closing in on her as she thought back to their previous conversations. She never really considered the possibility it could actually happen. "Oh, no. This can't be."

"I'm sorry to spring this on you today, but you weren't talking to me and I didn't want to push you. When I got your invitation to join you today, I assumed we would talk about it. It's an important next step for me."

"Oh," she whispered, feeling completely deflated. "How will this work? You are going to be consumed by your residency, and I will be tied to my work. Nate, I can't leave the company."

"I would never ask you to do that. I know how much the company means to you."

"Why can't you stay here? I need you here with me! I can't do a long-distance relationship."

"There isn't a pediatric surgical residency here. The one that accepted me is the most prestigious in the country. Think of what that would do for my career. Victoria . . ." he pleaded while she shook her head back and forth. The prospect of losing Nate now, combined with the deep loss of her father. She felt like her emotions would swamp her.

With one hand, he held up his sweater and undershirt, and with his other hand, he took her chin and gently lifted her head up. As her eyes tracked up from the bench, she could see what he was showing her. With her hand, she reached out, touching his bare chest. Using her index finger, she slowly traced the outline of multiple scars. The reminders of the surgeries of his childhood. He took his hand and held hers as she traced the scars.

"This is who I was meant to be."

A few tears escaped her eyes, and sadness flowed over her. On this bright sunny day, her dreams were being taken away. But how could she be mad? He was following his dream. It would be so incredibly selfish of her to insist he change his plans. She removed her hand from his chest.

"I feel so lost," she whispered, and he held her hand in a futile attempt to comfort her. "I'm sorry, Nate. I don't think I can do this." She hugged him, stood up, and began walking away, not sure if she would ever be able to overcome the disappointment she had been handed. As their hands separated, Nate begged her to stay and talk.

"Please, Victoria. We can figure this out. Give it a chance." She was numb as she walked back to her car, convinced that she must be a terrible person to have so much go wrong in her life in such a short time.

***

"Hi, Ms. Van Hough. What can I get for you tonight?" the young bartender asked.

"I'll take a bourbon sour."

"You got it," the bartender replied as he gathered the ingredients to make her drink. "I haven't seen you in a while, so I wanted to tell you how sorry I am about the loss of your father. He was a good man. I miss seeing you guys here."

"Thanks, Jack. That's nice of you to say. It's been hard coming back here without him." Jack was the afternoon bartender at the 19th hole, the first-floor bar at the country club where her family had a membership for many years. She didn't like golf, or even understand it, but came here frequently with her father. She always wondered why anyone would want to chase that little white ball around in the blazing heat. Regardless, she enjoyed the food and occasionally used the pool. Strangely enough, her father didn't play golf, either. But the list of members here was a who's who of local wealth, power, and society, so he felt it was important to have a presence here.

Jack set the glass on the bar and Victoria took a small sip, savoring the taste of the bourbon. Not as good as what they import at Van Hough Industries, but not bad. She had been trying to get them to buy their bourbon for a long time, without success. She looked around. The bar looked like something from a time capsule with decor more suitable for the 1970s. Along the back wall, she could see out to the eighteenth green with a wide asphalt path and space to park golf carts near the door. Frequently, golfers briefly parked their carts there, coming in for a cocktail before continuing with their game. The door flew open and two middle-aged men came in. Their shirts were soaked and the smell of their sweat mixed with cigars made Victoria almost gag. She picked up her drink and took a seat at a table near the windows. Here, she could be alone with her thoughts.

The events from today were still overwhelming, and she felt like a dark cloud had settled over her. The most frustrating part of the situation was that no one was wrong. It was so much easier when that wasn't the case. You felt better when you could place blame somewhere. Instead, this was the unsatisfactory feeling you got from a tie or a draw. Nate wasn't wrong. He had spent most of his life dreaming of being a pediatric surgeon, and now he had the chance. How could Victoria ask him to forego that? And, in her opinion, she wasn't wrong, either. She wanted a lasting relationship with a man she could love and who would love her back. All indications were that Nate was the man. But that wasn't possible now. Nate's dream would take him two thousand miles away, and Victoria was not a long-distance-relationship girl. No matter how strong her feelings were for Nate, she couldn't see how it would work out. The thought made her even more sad. She took another sip of her drink and fought to keep the tears from falling.

The noise was increasing as the remaining golfers were coming in to have drinks and food before going home. Victoria appreciated the distraction since the activity helped keep her mind occupied on other things besides Nate. The sun was at the perfect angle to make it difficult to see outside, so Victoria turned to people-watch those at the bar.

There didn't seem to be anything scandalous going on, so she sipped her drink. Over the past few years, when she was old enough to recognize it, she often picked out people she knew were doing things that society frowned upon. Her father always told her to not be overly interested in other people's business or you risk them taking an interest in yours. Of course, he was right, but it was so much fun.

"Victoria?"

The sound of her name startled her, and she snapped her head around to see who it was. The sun shone in her eyes, temporarily blinding her until she raised her hand to shield them. Her heart sank.

"Carter?"

"Hi. I didn't expect to find you here. What are you up to?"

"Just relaxing before I go home."

As she finished, Victoria saw another figure move in to stand next to Carter. She adjusted her seat so she could see both she and Carter without being blinded by the sun. Carter's new golf partner was a beautiful woman in her twenties and dressed fashionably in a pink golf shirt and matching short skirt.

"*Tu es pret, ma chere?*" she asked, then realized her mistake. "I'm so sorry," she said, her French accent very heavy. "I'm not accustomed to speaking English." Looking down at Victoria, she asked, "Carter, who is dis?" with obvious emphasis on *dis*, and Victoria had to fight to keep from rolling her eyes.

Victoria extended her hand, but before she could reciprocate, Carter whisked her away toward the bar. "Sorry, dear, they are calling us to our table." And without another word, they shuffled away.

Before she could even give Carter a second thought, she was consumed again by Nate. How did this go so wrong? How would she ever fill the void in her life? The despair was back, full force.

CHAPTER THIRTEEN

Music played softly in the background as Victoria typed away on her keyboard. She loved orchestral music. It calmed her and helped her to stay centered. At this most trying time for her, she needed every tool she could get. She had texted with Nate a handful of times, but it only made things worse for her. She made it clear to him, without trying to influence his decision, that she wasn't interested in a long-distance relationship. He was so sweet, patient, and understanding, and she loved that about him. But he was still leaving. She looked up at the clock on her desk and saw it was nearly four o'clock. His flight would take off in thirty minutes, and she was a wreck. If she could only concentrate on her work, things would be much better. She reached for her phone and turned up the music. Cymbals crashed as the London Symphony Orchestra played Handel's Messiah. With the volume of her sound system up to seventy, she was sure the entire estate was listening with her. Her head bobbed in time to the music as she opened her laptop to review emails from work. She had 260. "Damn, doesn't anyone take a weekend off?" she said as she scanned down the list, determining which ones she was in the mood to read. After reading two and responding to another, she realized it was not going as she hoped.

In an attempt to distract herself, she picked up her cell phone and started scrolling through her news apps. The vibration of her phone was startling, causing it to drop from her hands to the ground. She picked it up and saw a text from Sue.

Hey Vic! How are you doing? I was just thinking about you and decided to text.

Victoria knew she was trying to test the waters. They had talked a lot over the past few days and she knew Nate was leaving today. Undoubtedly, she was concerned about her friend. She texted back: Thanks for your concern, but I'm doing fine today. Nothing I can do about it anyway. She hit Send and put her phone back on the desk. She quickly checked the clock and hated herself for doing it. Only fifteen minutes until he flew out of her life. She took a deep breath, then went back to reading emails. She scanned the list again, finding one from an important coffee supplier in Columbia marked urgent. He was warning them of some political unrest that may impact the next shipment of coffee beans. They needed her to call first thing Monday morning. She took her phone and placed a reminder in it.

Then another text from Sue. I was thinking. I'm out running errands, so I'm going to stop by and see you.

"Oh, no." Victoria had been lazy all day and was still in her nightshirt and shorts. But to be honest, she could use a friend right now, so she didn't mind getting a little cleaned up. She texted back asking how long and Sue said about thirty minutes. She would text her when she was pulling up.

The sound system transitioned from Messiah to Vivaldi's The Four Seasons as she ran into her closet, gathered up some clothes, and took them to the bathroom for a shower. Normally, Victoria's showers were legendary, but not today. After putting her hair up, she got in, taking just enough time to wash her body. Ten minutes later, she was out, getting dressed and brushing her hair at her makeup table. Makeup? Oh, what the heck. Maybe a little.

After all, who was she trying to impress?

She knew she shouldn't, but she snuck a peek at the clock and her heart sunk. It was 4:35, and she pictured him in his seat as the plane barreled down the runway for an on-time departure. The thought made her a little nauseous, and she covered her face with her hands and propped her elbows on the table. She tried to fight back tears but was unsuccessful. This was going to take some time to get over, and she was just going to have to accept that she would have some bad days until then. She looked at herself in the mirror, wiped away her tears, and examined the small bags under her eyes. "Ugh."

After spending the next ten minutes putting on a splash of makeup, she was satisfied she could face her friend. Her phone vibrated and the text from Sue read: Be there in five. Meet me outside. She put her phone down and walked over to the window, looking outside. It was raining. Perfect. The weather matches my mood. She used her phone to turn the sound system off, leaving an incredible quiet behind. The only thing she could hear was the gentle pattering of the rain against the window.

As she gathered her raincoat from her closet, she hoped that her mother didn't hear her walking around downstairs. She was the last person Victoria wanted to talk to. She decided to sneak down as quietly as possible, hoping to go undetected. But she knew that if Helen saw her, it would be game over.

She opened the door and snuck out into the hallway, slowly making her way to the front door. Down the long hallway she went until she got to the stairs, which she descended with catlike stealth. Then, a right to the front door and she was home free, releasing her breath that she had been holding as she grasped the doorknob.

"Ms. Victoria. You may want to take this umbrella with you. It's raining outside." The sound of Helen's voice caused Victoria to jump, and she released her grip on the knob to turn around. Behind her was, as expected, Helen with an umbrella in her extended hand. She stepped forward, taking it from her.

"Thank you, Helen," she said as she turned back toward the front door, listening for the sound of Helen's footsteps as they carried away down the hallway. She opened the door and stepped out onto the front portico. She turned back to the house to make sure the door was closed before opening the umbrella and turning back toward the driveway. She took two steps forward and froze in her tracks. "What the heck is going on?"

With surprising agility, she dropped her umbrella and sprinted across the porch, springing over the two steps leading to the driveway. After splashing through several puddles, she leapt straight into Nate's arms, knocking him back against his car, causing his umbrella to fly out of his hand and skid across the cobblestone driveway.

She planted a firm kiss on his lips and gave him a bear hug, wrapping her legs around his torso and refusing to let him go. "What are you doing here? You're supposed to be on an airplane?" she asked as the rain ran down her face. If she was being honest, it wasn't all rain on her face, but she was thankful to have something else to blame.

He gently set her down, reaching for her hood, and pulled it up over her head to protect her from the rain. He slid his hand inside the hood, cupping her face gently. "I couldn't do it, Victoria. I couldn't leave you."

"But your residency. You are going to be late."

"I'm not going," he said, and the words landed hard on her heart.

"No! You have to go. It's your dream, Nate! I can't be responsible for you not following your dream," she said and started to cry.

"Victoria, please listen. This was one hundred percent my decision. You shouldn't have any guilt," he said as the rain soaked his hair and ran down his face. "You were right, we are perfect for each other. I spent every day thinking about your laugh, and your gentle touch, and your wonderful sense of humor. I miss the feel of your soft skin, and your body against mine. I asked myself, what if we only get a single chance to capture love? What would I do if it was standing right in front of me and I let it go? I want to find out. Are you my destiny? My soul mate? Do you want to find out, too?"

"Yes!" she yelled into the rain-soaked air. "I want to try! But what about your residency?" she asked again.

"I decided to put it off for a year. It will be there, Victoria. It will be there next year, but I didn't want to take a chance that you wouldn't be. I couldn't live with myself if I let this opportunity pass us by."

Victoria pulled him close again into a tight embrace, then looked up to the sky, closing her eyes and letting the rain fall gently on her face. She knew that somewhere up there, her father was looking down on them, and he was pleased. He had a hand in this, and she knew it.

"Thanks, Dad."

AFTERWORD

Thank you so much for reading my book! I hope you enjoyed it. If so, maybe you would consider doing me a favor. Reviews matter to authors like me. Please leave a review for me.

If you are interested in getting information about upcoming release dates for future books in this series or others, or if you would like to learn more about me or subscribe to my newsletter, visit my website at:

http://www.raemerson.com

You can connect with me by sending an email here:

info@raemerson.com

Thank you again!!

ABOUT THE AUTHOR

Hi! My name is Robert Emerson, and I love writing Contemporary Romance novels. But it wasn't always about writing. In fact, being an author is one of many careers I've enjoyed during my working life. Over that time, I've worked as a cook, a printer, an Operations Manager and a Registered Nurse to name just a few. Each job has helped me create a rich pool of experiences that I can draw from to write deep and engaging characters. I'm a romantic at heart and enjoy writing stories of love, trial, betrayal and redemption.

For the last few years, I have lived with my wife, in a 320 square foot tiny house on wheels. We travel the country, seeing beauty around us, and of course, I use these experiences to enhance my novels. We have five children between us who are all grown adults. Instead of pets, we have a cactus.

I love hearing from my readers so feel free to drop me an email, sign up for my newsletter or follow me on social media. Thank you all!